To Mary

Letters To My Sister
Volume 2

by
Janice Monahan Rodgers

Janice Monahan Rodgers

To Mom and Dad

"The best parents in the world"

May HIS light shine upon you both forever

Your Loving Daughter,

Jannie

TABLE OF CONTENTS

INTRODUCTION

Like the first "Letters To My Sister", this second volume "Chew Street and Beyond" is a collection of short stories that take place during the late 1940's and early 1950's in and around the city of Allentown, Pennsylvania.

It chronicles my family's vacations, our adventures in our Chew Street neighborhood and our big move to the 'suburbs' in a nostalgic, funny and sentimental fashion.

Postwar Allentown was, at the time, a thriving, growing community. A third-class city of the Commonwealth of Pennsylvania, its population of over 106,000 people was becoming quite diverse but it still held a strong Pennsylvania German attachment.

Names like Trexler, Ritter, Wetherhold, Fenstermaker, Merkel, Roth and Ruhe rubbed elbows with the likes of Cappellini, Monahan, Chernensky, Egan, Lesko, Mitchell, Munchak and Lomonski.

My siblings and I grew up at a time in this country's history when a post wartime economy was rapidly changing our world.

We shopped at Hess's, Leh's or the Zollinger Harned Company and all the stores in between from Fifth and Hamilton to Tenth and Hamilton Streets. We went to the movies at the Colonial, Rialto, Earle or Boyd theaters.

We had steak sandwiches at the Look Lunch and tried a new kind of sandwich called a hoagie at Woolworth's.

We rode trolley cars, saw the inception of the first television sets, marveled at a first trip to a '*supermarket*', and were heavily influenced by 'television commercials' for everything from toothpaste to breakfast cereals. We played games with neighborhood kids and climbed a jungle gym at the local park.

We made new friends and learned diplomacy and when that didn't work, we figured out how to stand our ground and occasionally, fight for our rights.

We saw how new technology was beginning to impact our lives. We were living in some of the most exciting times in the twentieth century but didn't realize then how important those changes would be to our future.

Throughout all those days, months and years growing up in Allentown, a fine golden thread was woven inextricably in the tapestry of our young lives binding us to our church, our family and our friends, old and new.

I hope these gentle and nostalgic stories will entertain you, dear reader. Perhaps it will trigger fond memories of your own or for my younger readers, spur an interest in what it was like growing up *back in those days*.

Enjoy!

Janice Monahan Rodgers

THE PERM

I threw myself across the bed and sobbed my heart out. I was seven years old and my life was over. I was doomed. Doomed to a life of pathetic wretchedness. Done in by Marcel Grateau and Karl Nessler! They had pretty much ruined my life, probably forever.

Who were Marcel and Karl, you ask, and what did a Frenchman and a German have to do with my wretchedness?

Well, in 1872, a Frenchman named Marcel Grateau developed a heated curling rod so women could have curly or wavy hair anytime they liked. This process of curling hair was known as 'marcelling' and the waves it produced were known as 'marcels'.

Around 1905, a German named Karl Nessler took it a step further and developed a permanent wave machine, which were rods connected to a machine with an electric heating device, but, alas, it was only effective on long hair (since it was downright lethal on short hair). Along the way, Nessler improved upon his invention and, after some serious mishaps with burnt hair, he did find success.

Still you ask, what had all this to do with a seven year old girl in Pennsylvania?

Well, the sad tale as far as we in the family can recall, goes something like this.

For some ungodly reason, Mom decided that I should have a perm (also known as a permanent wave.) Since I already had naturally curly waves that Marcel and Karl's customers would have probably killed for, I will never know what motivated my mother to make this fateful decision, other than she wanted me to look like Shirley Temple.

The morning started out so promising. Mom and I had walked across the street to Pauline's Beauty Shop. I was really excited since only older ladies got perms. Usually, the only reason I ever went to the beauty parlor was to get my hair cut.

After I was ensconced on a booster seat, Pauline rolled out the permanent wave machine and plugged it into the wall outlet. It was a fearsome looking contraption with wires and rods that hung down from a canopy like the tentacles of a jellyfish.

One by one the rods were fitted onto my hair. It seemed to take forever until they were properly attached and I began to squirm as my legs stuck to the leather booster seat. Then a solution was applied to my hair strands that were coiled tightly in the rods. The stuff smelled to high heaven.

Finally, the machine was turned on and a slight humming emanated from the rods. The stink still stank! But I figured that's what it took for a perm. Assured that I would have lovely curls, and my hair would look beautiful, I endured the torture.

About an hour later or less, maybe, the timer buzzed, the machine was shut off and Pauline began to remove the rods. That's when I began to seriously worry. I couldn't turn my head this way and that, but I could still see that my normally loose waves were now seriously kinky. Pauline proceeded to comb out my hair and style it.

Was it my imagination, or were those formerly loose waves now boinging all over my head? The more she combed, the more they boinged! But they weren't soft, like before. No, these curls refused to uncurl. They were about to bring a new word into my vocabulary.

FRIZZ!

My hair had now taken on a life of its own. And it wasn't pretty. In fact, even though everyone was telling me how absolutely lovely it looked, I was more than a little uneasy.

Because my hair also *felt* funny too, like it was super thick and standing on end. No amount of smushing I did with my hands would make it lay down flatter.

I looked like Little Orphan Annie who just got a large charge –– of static electricity! I wanted to cry, to howl in anguish, but I was speechless.

THIS WAS A PERMANENT WAVE FOR GODSAKES! I could end up being like this forever! Oh, God!

But all the ladies at the beauty shop kept saying how *nice* it looked, so I remained mute as we left the shop. Mom and I crossed the street on a wave of ammonia and lacquer.

I immediately went upstairs to my bedroom and looked in the mirror. Maybe if I just ignored it, it would all go away, like a bad dream when the morning came. I didn't know it then, but the bad dream was about to turn into a nightmare.

Because, that's when my dad came in the front door.

"Where's Jannie?" I heard him ask Mom.

Nothing unusual in that. Dad was a cop and kept close tabs on his kids. He was always worrying about us since he saw all kinds of dreadful things happening to pitiful little neglected children.

The poor man had no idea of the horrific apparition that was about to greet him in his own domicile.

I gave my hair one last scrunch and went down to supper.

It's amazing how the human memory works. Like really, really bad events can be entirely forgotten over time. Oh Yeah! Well, not this one! Because, even after all these years, I can still remember the look on Dad's face when he saw me.

His eye widened. His handsome face went white. His jaw tightened. (This was not going to be good with the jaw tightening thing.) His face looked like he really could not fathom what he was seeing, but knew it was all too real. That this travesty had happened! In his own home! To his own child!

Then he turned his cold eyes on Mom.

"What in the name of God, Margaret, what *is* this?" he said with that sound of incredulity in his voice that he made when confronted with sheer stupidity.

That was when the dam broke. I started bawling and ran back up to my bedroom. I heard the commotion down below and sobbed while I considered my options. I could run away from home, or jump out of the window, or maybe join the circus. I am sure the circus would have room for a new act. I could be billed as Jannie, the Frizzy Haired Wonder. Maybe my boingy curls could be used to launch projectiles. It was obvious my own father could no longer bear to look at my mangled mane, my ruined tresses, my lacerated locks.

There was a terrible outburst from Mom and then another from Dad and then the quiet, controlled, icy voice of a man betrayed in his own home. By his very own loved ones!

"Margaret, don't you ever, ever do anything like that again to that child!"

With the snap of the evening newspaper, and the bang of a pot on the stove, my life was over!

The next day I got a new haircut, the idea being my hair would look less frizzy as the perm grew out. Luckily for me, I was the one child of his four that Dad had passed his thick wavy Irish locks on to, so no lasting damage was done.

As for the whole perm debacle, the unfortunate incident was never spoken of again. And – I didn't have to join the circus.

You know, there is one drawback to being the first child in a family of four kids. I was always the test case. Parents don't usually visit their mistakes onto their other children, so you, my dear sister, never had to endure looking like the bride of Frankenstein. Even for one night.

You would think that this horrifying event from my childhood would have so traumatized me, that I would never have undergone such a procedure again. Ha! Not hardly. Decades later, after time had somewhat dimmed my memory, I decided I would get a curly perm. It was all the rage, even guys were doing it.

When I swanned into the house with my curly new Harpo-esque locks, Dad took one look at me, laughed and said, "Jannie, you look like one of Mary Cherry's girls."

This remark may not have fazed anyone else, but I knew the reference. Besides saving pitiful neglected children, as an officer of the law, Dad often had to arrest ladies of the evening. You got it. Mary Cherry's girls.

I got my hair cut and waited for the perm to grow out!

Ah well, who said life was ever going to be easy.

I am sure Mr. Nessler didn't have an easy time of it either, when he first invented his machine. I can see him now, beating it down the alleys of Bremerhaven with a portmanteau full of rollers, as hordes of angry women with singed hair pursue him to the docks, yelling SCHWEINEHUND!

Authors Note:

Our hairdresser, Pauline, was a gentle, sweet, kind woman. She continued to cut and style my hair for many, many years. On my wedding day, there was no one else I would allow to touch my hair. God bless you, Pauline B. You were a treasure.

WINTER DAYS ON CHEW STREET

I've always had a love/hate relationship with winter. It dates back to my early childhood days when wintertime on Chew Street could alternately be a fairyland of white fluff or a stinging, arctic tundra, sometimes all in the same day!

While the winter months offered a host of holidays we kids adored, they were often accompanied by bitter, bleak days. Starting with Thanksgiving in November, and its early onset of frosty days, polar December soon rolled in with its promise of Christmas parties, Santa Claus and presents. But even this couldn't mitigate the harshness of a stinging January wind as we kids walked backwards up the street to Immaculate Conception School. February with its gushy valentines stole our breath while we plowed through slushy streets on our way home from school clutching those special Valentines. March, buffeted us from side to side when we tried to play in the school yard canyon created by the convent on one side and our tall three story school building on the other.

What follows, dear sister, is an example of a few snowy days on Chew Street, long, long ago!

The very first snowstorm of the season was pure magic to me as a child. Happy memories of sledding with my pals, of sipping hot cocoa after a day in the snow, of standing on the heating register thawing out, of being snug and warm in our little row house; this was the love part of wintertime for me.

That morning the lowering skies held a promise. Sure enough, snowflakes, crystalline and pure, began to flutter down, coating the stark black branches of the chestnut tree in front of our little row house. As I watched from our living room window, the snow soon covered the herringbone brick pavement, parked cars and then the street. They were magical crystals, turning everything in my small vista into a frosty, arctic whiteness. As though some winter fairy took her glacial wand and turned my bleak world into a wonderland of white fluff.

It wasn't long before Mr. Steiner, the next door neighbor, came out to put chains on his truck. That meant the snow storm was going to be a deep one, I figured. Oh, goody! Even better, today was Saturday!

I watched the old paperhanger/painter perform his winter mission. With the preciseness with which he performed every task, the old gentleman laid out the chains behind his rear tires, jockeyed his truck back on them, hooked the links in place, and Voila, it was done. He was ready to roll. So was I.

Like a prearranged signal, I tore down the cellar steps to look for my sled and then scurried back up to haul my black goodyear boots out of the back of the closet behind the cellar door. Now all I had to do was wait for mountains of snow to accumulate!

There was always a sense of urgency to our preparations when snow fell. Because sadly, for us kids anyway, snowstorms in the city didn't stay white and pristine for long. Before we knew it, folks would shovel their sidewalks and then spread the ashes from their coal furnaces so people wouldn't slip and fall, thus spoiling all of our fun. Delivery trucks soon appeared plowing through the streets, turning the white snow dirty and slushy. So we needed to make the most of the time we had while praying for a good deep snow.

Since the streets in our neighborhood, like Chew Street, could sometimes be busy with traffic, I usually sledded on the sidewalk in front of our house with

Helen, Cappy, Dolly and a few other kids. Our half block of Chew Street was a nice downward slope. Great for sledding right into the loading dock of the factory at the bottom of our hill.

As the snow fell faster and deeper that day, we were having a fine old time. After falling off our sleds at the loading dock and rolling in the snow, we looked, for all intents and purposes, like snowmen ourselves. The heavy snow stuck to our clothes like white glue, settling in cracks and crevices of our leggings and jackets.

As the day snowed on, we decided to expand our sledding adventures to include Railroad Street, since it had the least traffic and was a lengthier hill. Although, some of the kids on that street could be a tad rowdy and territorial. However, we overlooked that minor obstacle until things got too rough. Whereupon, my friends and I retreated posthaste to my backyard.

A heavy, deep snow also meant an opportunity to make great snow caves in our teeny back yard and a pygmy snow man or two. That day, the wet snow packed like cement. For those of us with more artistic leanings, it allowed us to give our creativity free reign (without interference from roughnecks). Our backyards often became our refuge.

After an enjoyable afternoon playing in the snow, which by now had to be at least two feet deep, Mom called. Time for my pals to go home and me to go in.

I took my wet jacket and leggings down to the basement and hung them in front of the coal fired furnace. In the warm, toasty basement, they dried out in no time, ready for the next round of play.

Mom already had my cocoa ready for me. She made the best hot cocoa using Hershey's cocoa, milk and a little sugar. It warmed me right down to my frozen toes (I must say, no one ever made hot cocoa as good as my mom.) When bed time came, I slept like a log.

However, there were also several drawbacks to the good, old deep snowstorms of my childhood.

This is where the hate part of my wintertime memories looms large.

Drawback Number One

Monday - School and Getting Dressed for the Joyless Journey

Firstly, and of paramount importance, the term 'snow days' was not in our vernacular when I was a kid. Snow days simply meant, hey, it was *snowing*. It did NOT mean that school was canceled. Why? Because, we all walked to school, that's why! So, there was no excuse for not coming to school. Besides, we also had trolley cars, *with snow catchers on them.*

Now, after a weekend of enjoying the fluffy stuff, Monday had frostily rolled around with lowering, leaden skies. The weekend's several feet of accumulated snow, was now getting a bit slushy and icy. Although, no new flakes fell that morning, the air held that quiet stillness that preceded another heavy snowfall.

My school was three blocks away. I was not looking forward to the trip. Because it meant trudging through banks of deep cinder splotched snow, *uphill — both ways.* At least, that's how it felt to me.

Preparations for my trek to school were equally burdensome. It took me a good ten minutes just to get outfitted like Nanook of the North for the expedition.

First, came a pair of woolen leggings. Stuffing myself and my plaid school dress into them one leg at a time while hopping around and then snapping the suspenders, took most of my energy. Next, I had to put on a sweater since our class room could be drafty.

Once this was accomplished, I sat down and proceeded to push my Buster Brown shoes into my boots and clamp them shut. Once fastened, the cumbersome clamps defied any effort of my small puny fingers to get them *unclamped* once I got into the cloakroom at school.

Lastly, came my jacket, hat, mittens and of course, my scarf, which covered half my face. Weighed down now by a preponderance of wool, I could barely pick up my school bag. I slowly proceeded to the front door where an icy blast greeted me as I stepped out onto the front stoop. (Yeah, I know, none of this bothered me when I was going out to play. Get over it!)

But this was just the beginning of the torturous journey for which I prepared. A route that was fraught with any manner of trials, tribulations and danger, now stretched perilously before me!

Danger? Perils? Trials? Why, you ask? Because of…

Drawback Number Two.

Snowball Battles.

On my trek through the frozen wasteland that was Ridge Avenue, I needed to pass through several checkpoints (snow ball throwing zones). This morning, *going to* school wasn't a problem with the so-called checkpoints. Because the felonious snow ball throwers were on their way to school too and most wouldn't have time to launch a full scale attack.

Coming home was the problem. The fiends had time on their side to get to their embattlements and prepare.

That day school left out at the regular time, 3:00 pm. I put on my Nanook gear, wrapped my scarf around my face and squared my shoulders. I had been down this road before. Literally. I departed the cloakroom with a gaggle of other kids. It was time to meet the *enemy.*

Checkpoint one came early on – a quarter of a block from the school yard.

The rules were –- there were no rules!

It was every man (or woman) for himself.

Unfortunately for me, I had a terrible pitching arm. Plus, my snowballs were beyond lame. I never seemed to pack them right and they went nowhere. They just fizzed out in a blur of white.

So this left me with only one defense. Run like hell through the blitzkreig and hope that there would be minimal damage inflicted.

It didn't take me long to become what I called a defensive runner. I learned to move like a corkscrew decanting a bottle of bubbly. (Self-preservation is a great motivator and ballet dancing lessons helped too.)

I set off at a clip! Twist and run, block with my school bag and run, jump behind a telephone pole and block, then *just* run — like blazes! I even put in a few ballet moves; a leap here, a glissade there, then jete and arabesque over a snow pile.

Incredibly, I managed to get through unscathed, uh, excluding my school bag. I had pretty much run the gamut of all checkpoints, and was feeling rather pleased with myself.

But I was about to learn two lessons. Don't count your snowballs until they're thrown or *it ain't over til it's over*. And, never underestimate the value of high drama.

By the time I reached Chew Street, I slowed down. I was out of breath from my death defying run. Most of the activity at the checkpoints was over. It was getting too darned cold to be out in the snow, anyway. Even for the delinquents on Ridge Avenue.

I was feeling pretty good. My front porch stoop was in view. Almost home. As I neared my friend Cappy's house, I was daydreaming of hot cocoa and cookies. I could almost taste them.

But in my euphoria, I had forgotten — *The scourge of Railroad Street! The Flynn Brothers!*

Without warning, from behind Gogle's car, BLAM! A double whammy of icy snowballs hit me square in the middle of my back, propelling me forward. I went down in the snow like a ten pin in a bowling alley.

You know, no one likes to be blindsided. (To this day, it ticks me off when that happens to me.)

But this time, I was seriously ticked. Not to mention, damn, it hurt. Because, I knew immediately who the devils were. I could hear their demonic laughter behind me. *Stinking Flynns!*

Tears welled in my eyes. I had two choices. I could run home crying, which actually seemed like a pretty good idea at the time. But since I just ran all the way down Ridge Avenue, I was kind of tired.

Or I could use another tactic and hoped it worked. Should I give it a whirl? I was probably going to get hammered anyway.

I chose the latter.

Slowly, I got up and turned to face my tormentors.

"Jimmy Flynn, you are a skunk. I hate your skunky guts! You're gonna be sorry too, Tommy. Just you wait and see!"

Their demonic laughter and taunts of crybaby filled the arctic air as they prepared to lob another volley of their glacial ammunition at me.

A quick glance into Cappy's front window showed his Mom dusting her piano. Perfect! A witness! Oh, this was gonna be so good.

I edged closer and closer to her window. All the time, I kept my eyes trained on Jimmy's right arm. The fiend had a mean fast ball. I waited till he dipped and reached back.

Then I let it rip. Taking a deep breath, I began to scream bloody murder. In the still, frigid air, my shrieks resounded as though Murder Incorporated itself was on Cappy's doorstep. My screams of torment and agony bounced off of Gogle's car and reverberated around the frigid air above the Flynn Brothers' dimwitted heads.

Jimmy Flynn's red ears and face turned white. Tommy's mouth dropped along with the two ice-packed snowballs he was getting ready to hurl.

As my anguished screams hung in the frozen atmosphere, Cappy's Mom, bless her heart, ran out her front door with a broom and chased the Flynn's half way up the street.

I picked up my school bag and allowed her to escort me and my tear stained cheeks to my front door.

Glancing over my shoulder, I watched the Flynns beating it up Railroad Street and - -smiled.

My performance was academy award worthy. Why, I hardly even worked up a sweat! Sarah Bernhardt, that celebrated queen of drama and death scenes, had nothing on me. My thespian histrionics were pitch-perfect, so to speak.

I thanked Mrs. Cappy's mom for my rescue and opened my front door to the smell of hot cocoa wafting from the kitchen.

"How was school today, honey?" Mom asked as I came in the door.

"Pretty good, Mom," I replied.

Smiling to myself, I figured any day I put one over on the Flynn brothers was a pretty good day.

Never underestimate the power of a woman, Jimmy Flynn. Especially one who knows how to act! Ah, the theatah, the theatah...

HOW THE MAD RUSSIAN MET THE ENFORCER

My mother was a gentle, sweet soul. She was always doing nice things for her family and friends. Like crocheting an afghan for someone in need or baking goodies for friends or neighbors. (It was a known fact that our parish priest, Father McGonigle, often saved his neighborhood visits until Mom's baking day.)

The seventh of nine children, her childhood was extremely harsh by today's standards. Taken out of school and put to work in a factory when she was only twelve, she would have had every reason to be bitter about her lot in life. Instead she simply saw the best in everyone. Probably because of the ugliness that surrounded her for all those years, she hated confrontations of any kind. She hated arguments, she hated fighting, and she hated bullies. She generally practiced what she preached, but she knew sometimes an altercation was inescapable. However, her mantra, to me at least, was always, "Now Jannie, be nice."

In that last respect, as a child, I was very much like her. I too disliked confrontations and unpleasantness and tried to avoid them as often as possible. They sucked too much of the joy and energy out of life.

My Dad was a charming and handsome man. However, he also had a reputation for being *extremely* just and fair. (Great qualities, since he was a police officer.) Although, when dealing with the rambunctious four that were his children, he was known, on occasion to "blow his stack". But he was *always* fair when administering punishment.

Nevertheless, that very strong sense of justice, knowing what was right and doing it, no matter the cost, was at his very core. It was who he was. He could no more deny it than stop breathing. He could not bear to see an injustice being committed. Nor would he ever back down from a fight when it involved the violation of his or others' rights. In that last respect, you, my dear sister, were very much like him. Even at the tender age of not quite five.

So what follows, my dear sister, is a tale of injustice. A story involving an umbrella, a golf club (putter to be exact) and a mad Russian. A narrative of familial devotion and loyalty. A saga of felonious assault, theft and just plain meanness. Lastly, the means by which justice was fairly (and swiftly) administered.

The conflict began innocently enough when our dear Aunt Rita came to visit bearing gifts. Aunt Ree, as we in the family called her, was Dad's older sister and she was one of our favorite relatives. She took us to movies, out to lunch, shopping in downtown Allentown and brought us gifts. Never married, with no children of her own, she spoiled us rotten.

On this particular day, she showed up with a bonanza; a big bag of candy, an umbrella (kid size) for me and a golf club and golf ball for my little sister. I remember how proud I was to have my very own umbrella, whereupon I got all kinds of lectures from Mom about not opening it in the house because that was bad luck. Also, I should take good care of it because it wasn't a toy, etc, etc., etc.

The toy golf club had a red wooden shaft with a silver aluminum putting wedge on the end. The club and ball was affixed to a giant cardboard that we lost no time in tearing apart. It didn't take long for Kathy, to run out into the backyard to try out the club after a lecture from Mom about how to swing (low), where *not* to aim (neighbors windows), etc, etc, etc.

I joined her out there, swanning around and twirling my new acquisition like Gene Kelly on a dry day, while she pretended to be the new Sammy Snead.

Now in the melting pot that was the first and sixth wards of our city, lived all kinds of kids. Most of the time, we all got along and played well. But there was one kid, who defied the norm.

Peter Tischenko, or as we in the hood called him, the Mad Russian. Peter was tall for his eleven years, and muscular. He had thin, sandy colored hair and green eyes that kind of looked right through you. Think Vladmir Putin on steroids. (By the way, did you know that Vladimir means peaceful ruler and Putin means road. Yeah, just sayin'. Make of it what you will.)

Anyway, Tischenko didn't have too many friends, due to the fact that those who tried to befriend him generally ended up with a fat lip. Peter was a lone wolf, no pun intended. The Mad Russian nomenclature came mostly from his mother, who was constantly yelling or arguing with someone about something. The woman never looked happy, ever!

Peter on the other hand, continually wore a bland, rather cold expression. You never could tell if he was happy, sad, mad or what he might do next. Peter made my neighborhood nemeses, the Flynns, look like altar boys (well, which they were actually.) On my sporadic run-ins with the Flynns, they were just obnoxious. But Peter was a bully, and a mean one.

So, most of us just gave him a wide berth. If we saw him coming, we walked the other way.

Well, that day, somewhere along the line, I decided to pop on over to see my friend Helen and show off my new red 'brolly'. I slipped out of the yard through our alley way, went around the corner and turned down onto Railroad Street where it was my great misfortune to run smack into the Mad Russian.

Caught by surprise, I felt like a deer caught in the headlights of his myopic, green stare.

"Where're *you* goin?" he asked in a flat voice.

"To, to Helen's." I answered, somewhat shakily. I tried sidestepping the thug, but he quickly stepped in front of me again.

"What's that?" he asked pointing to my new umbrella.

I was seven and had not yet developed my now infamous wise cracking mouth, so there was no sharp retort coming from me. Also, he was twice my size, so braining him with my new umbrella wasn't even an option. I figured if I could keep him engaged in a conversation, I could get past him and run like blazes for home.

"It's my new umbrella. My Aunt bought it for me," I said, trying to appear friendly.

"Oh, yeah! Well, now it's mine," he growled and made a grab for it.

Then a scuffle and tug of war began. Struggling, I twisted and held on to it while he tried to wrest it from my grasp. The more he tugged, the more I pulled. Finally, he gave it a good wrench, I lost my footing and tripped on the curb, banging my elbow and knees. The fiend took advantage of my fall, grabbed it and hauled butt down the street.

Running home crying and sobbing, I tore into the house and flung myself on the sofa. There would be no, "Well, we'll just get you another one," appeasement from Mom. Money was tight in our house in those days. My new umbrella was gone forever, now racing down Railroad Street, clutched in the greasy paws of the Mad Russian.

While Mom tended my brush burns and tried to console me, neither of us noticed that the Sammy Snead newbie was missing. So was her new golf club.

Not too many minutes later, the phone rang. It was the Mad Russian's mother.

Actually, she needn't have bothered using the phone. People could probably hear her all over Railroad Street on up to Chew Street and beyond.

I remember seeing Mom's astonished face through my tear filled eyes when she answered. The conversation went something like this.

"That's impossible. My daughter is right here," Mom answered, detailing the recent fracas that resulted in my injuries and umbrella loss. "She could not possibly have beat up your son."

There was some more conversation on the other end of the phone line as the Mad Russian's Mom spoke to her whining son and clarified the true identity of his attacker.

"That's ridiculous," Mom retorted, looking at me. "Kathy's not even five years old and your son is twice her size.

Covering the receiver she whispered, "Where's Kathy?" I hiccupped and shrugged my shoulders in the universal sign for "don't have a clue".

"Indeed!" Mom continued as the Mad Russian's Mom wailed through the phone. "Well, I'll just have my husband come down there and have a chat with your son *and you*, when he gets off duty from the *police department*."

The line went dead.

Suddenly, the screen door banged and Kathy, the Sammy Snead newbie, appeared holding my battered umbrella in one hand and a broken golf club in the other. The club's wedge was dented and the shaft was split up the middle. She, on the other hand, looked just fine. Not a scratch on her.

Mom was just floored. That her tiny little girl could or even would take on the Mad Russian.

But even though Mom detested fighting of any kind, she knew Peter had needed a good drubbing for a long time. The fact that he finally got it from her sylph-like, not quite five year old, and a little girl at that, astounded my Mom. It had to be mortifying for Peter.

For days after the incident, Peter was conspicuously absent from his usual haunts. Apparently word of his humiliation traveled around the hood like wildfire. His bully creds evaporated like a rain puddle in the hot sun! We could now roam around our neighborhood, without fear of intimidation, thanks to my teeny baby sister.

Seems that when she saw me return from my altercation, her 'justice meter' spiked and she snuck out of the back yard on her self-appointed mission. Overcome with fury at the unfairness of what she had just witnessed, she decided to administer her own *justice.*

Her status in the hood rose overnight as someone *not* to be trifled with. (Probably a little fear was mixed in there too!) Funny how a conk on the head with a golf club can earn you respect — and by extension, the rest of us Monahan kids. So the *golf club incident*, as it came to be known, provided us with a measure of security and esteem in neighborhood circles for quite some time.

When I think back on it now, I picture my fragile little sister bearing down on the big lummox that was the Mad Russian. In my mind's eye, it's kind of like St. Michael the Archangel swooping down with his lightning swift sword! Peter never knew what was coming. I can see him now, standing there, laughing and taunting a teeny little girl, as she suddenly grew nine feet tall and beat the snot out of him.

As for the Mad Russians, they continued to maintain a very low profile and never gave us any trouble again. Particularly Peter.

Over the years, the ward as it was known, produced doctors, nurses, lawyers, police chiefs (Dad and my brother Jerry were two), priests, nuns, ministers, authors, teachers, CEO'S, and a myriad of professionals too numerous to mention here. It also yielded hard working folks who helped build this country in those post war years. Like shop and store owners, factory workers (my mom and aunts), office workers, health care workers (my Aunt Marie), beauticians (our neighbor Pauline), carpenters, steelworkers (my Uncle John), career military (my Uncle Joe) and so very many others, that made Allentown the Queen City it became.

I like to think that Peter finally became one of them. Perhaps a steelworker (he had the build for it) or a lawyer, or a postman or even a carpenter. Or maybe he became a child psychologist. Now wouldn't that be Freudian justice!

Because I am sure having the daylights walloped out of him by a five year old taught him more than old Sigmund ever could have.

As for the teeny enforcer, her sense of justice, fair play and honesty only increased over the years. In any conflict, she is the one person you want in your corner. She has always been in mine.

One thing though, we made certain we never taught her how to play golf after the *golf club incident.*

GAMBLERS ANONYMOUS

Chinchee Ma Chancha
Were the words that he said.
Gum balls rolled out,
Blue, green and red.

We were growing up. There were four of us kids in the Monahan clan now. While Jim was still a toddler, Jerry was old enough to accompany us on our travels around the neighborhood. Travels which often included a stop at Reimer's Grocery next door.

Mr. Reimer was ahead of his time as a promoter since he had cleverly placed the penny candy counter adjacent to the ice cream freezer with two gum ball machines between them. A stroke of genius on his part!

This nirvana was conveniently located right in the front of the store. No need to wade through canned asparagus or shelves of shoe polish to find our goodies.

I can see that candy counter like it was yesterday. Boxes of root beer barrels, watermelon slices, licorice sticks, and licorice pipes, vied for space with Mary Janes, BB Bats, Tootsie Rolls, wax soda bottles and wax lips, lollipops, gumdrops, chalky-sweet candy cigarettes, bubble gum cigars and more. The sweets beckoned like a siren of the sea, luring us onto the rocky shores of candy land.

Of course, all these goodies needed some cold hard cash to obtain. Something that was generally in short supply in our humble abode. (Even *after* we checked the sofa cushions for loose change)

Occasionally we would get lucky when Aunt Kitty, or Grandpop and Baba would give us some coins when we visited them. Personally, I always prayed for Baba to give me just a nickel or a quarter because, if she was really feeling generous, she would give us each a silver dollar. And my dear sister, as I am sure you will remember, Mom appropriated them immediately and put them in our banks where they were never seen again.

So, this presented a small dilemma. Yes, it had become all too evident. We lived next door to candy land. We had very little money to speak of. We needed to make what we did have, go further, last longer. We were in it for the long haul. Remember, we're talking pennies here.

It soon became crystal clear where our fortune lay, lie or laid.

Loaded with rainbow hued gumballs, the gumball machines soon became our favorite spot, our salvation so to speak.

"Why?" you ask.

Because, they weren't just purveyors of chewing gum. Oh no! They were cleverly disguised spherical games of chance. Slot machines for the pediatric set, if you will.

Yes, these sphere-shaped vendors of fruity goodness also contained special dotted, striped, silver and gold orbs, known as 'winners,' which when acquired, entitled the bearer to two cents (if you won the dotted), a nickel (if you won the striped), a dime (if you won the silver) or a quarter (if you won the gold). If you were lucky enough to score a winner, you were in the money.

With a neighborhood full of kids, this was true capitalism on Reimer's part. The man was way ahead of his time as a marketing genius. Plus, it also insured that the gum balls and candy were always fresh!

So, of course, being the shrewd and cunning strategists we kids were, it made perfect sense to try to increase our pennies by trying the gumball machines first. Even if you didn't win, you still got a gumball. A 'win-win' situation, I figured.

And here is where a charm called 'Chin Chee Ma Chancha' comes in.

We were standing in front of the gumball machine, Jerry, Kathy and I, trying to pool our meager resources.

"How much have you got?" I asked Kathy.

She pulled two pennies out of her pinafore pocket.

"What about you, Butch?" I asked, using the nickname we called him until he went to school.

Jerry reached down into his playsuit pocket and whipped out five pennies, slapping them down on the counter.

My mouth dropped. Now where on earth did he find five pennies? I had pretty much cleaned out the sofa only yesterday. Three years old and the kid's a walking bank!

Since he had the most money, we let him go first.

He popped his penny in the slot, and twisted the handle.

Then I heard him whisper, like a bedtime prayer – the weirdest words I ever did hear!

"Chinchee ma chancha!"

A two-cent winner rolled out.

What? Chinchee what?

Mr. Reimer gave him his two cents, and Jerry popped another penny in the gumball machine.

"Chinchee ma chancha, chinchee ma chancha," he warbled, giving the machine handle a good twist. Two silver orbs rolled out.

Mr. Reimer laughed and gave him two dimes.

I couldn't believe what I just saw – and heard.

The kid just won three winners. We were rich – or he was.
I looked down at my little brother in his blue play suit with his hair parted and slicked back and realized something. I was in the presence of greatness!

We picked out our candy, and Jerry pocketed his winnings for another day.

Now I do not have a clue where Jerry ever picked up the silly little charm. He just made it up, I guess. But it almost always worked for him. Of course, this was a kid who called his baby bottle of water 'howy' for the longest time so who knows what language he was speaking. Anyway, the gumball gods apparently heard him loud and clear.

Mr. Reimer, bless him, loved seeing Jerry come into the store to try his luck at the gumball machine. Jerry was eyeball to gumball height, as it were, and must have presented quite a picture as he prayed so gravely at the altar of the gumball machine reciting his 'Chinchee' prayer.

Almost every time he popped a penny in the slot, earnestly whispered the charm, twisted the handle, a winner would roll out! Man, he was always lucky, the little twit.

The winning was exciting enough, but Jerry would always parlay his winnings into a bigger bag of candy by buying 'two-fors.' You know, like two Tootsie Rolls for a penny or three watermelon slices for a penny, thus getting the biggest bang for his buck, or in his case, penny!

When we saw how it worked, we all tried it. (Even though I felt like an idiot reciting the charm. It sounded pretty lame to me!) But it always seemed to work best for Jerry. I guess you had to be on the same wave length as the gum ball gods.

Nonetheless, while we were chanting those silly little made up words (uttered with utmost conviction), they taught us some valuable lessons, in economics, investments, religion, social mores, and the like.

For instance, we learned that...

A penny saved is a penny earned (unless you're dumb enough to put them all in a gumball machine.)

We should always invest our earnings wisely.

We should plan our purchases just as carefully, ergo, two-fors will take you further!

Perhaps even more importantly –

There are some people who are just plain lucky, 'chinchees' notwithstanding!

Also, we learned (and Jerry learned this best) the 'power of positive thinking,' long before Norman Vincent Peale penned it for us!

But the wisest axiom we could take away from our early encounters with the gumball machines was this...

"Annual income, 20 pounds, Annual expenditure, 19 pounds. Result? Happiness."

Mr. Micawber – David Copperfield

And 'Chinchees' to Mr. Reimer, a kind and generous man. I'll never forget your store – especially the candy counter!

RAMAR OF THE JUNGLE

"Wow, Cappy, that's a neat ring," I said.

"Yeah, where did you get it?" Helen asked.

"Oh, it's from Captain Midnight. You know, on TV. It's a secret decoder ring. All you have to do is just watch the TV program and you can send in for one."

I groaned inwardly and just gave my friend Helen a sick look. She didn't have a TV set either. Crap! I could understand why Cappy had one though. He was an only child, plus he didn't have a father. Also, he was always getting into one scrape or another, so maybe his Mom figured that a TV would keep him occupied and out of trouble. I could have told her it wasn't working.

But I had a father *and* a mother. Neither of them seemed inclined to get a TV anytime soon. I said goodbye to my friends and trudged up Chew Street to my home.

"Jannie, please set the table," my mom said as I came in the backdoor.

"Mom, how come we can't have a TV like Susie and Cappy?" I whined as I plopped the dinner plates on the table. "I'm missing some great TV shows, like 'Captain Midnight' and 'The Cisco Kid'. I could even get a decoder ring with a manual and badge and everything."

Sadly, my TV viewing time at Susie's was strictly limited to 'Willie the Worm' and his cartoons and 'Western Theater', where they showed neat westerns with Bob Steele and Lash LaRue. Mom wasn't happy with even that much time. She didn't like to impose on the neighbors. Personally, I didn't mind. I liked Willie and his invisible sidekick, Newton the Mouse, even if you never ever saw Newton. It was all about the mystery of what Newton might look like. I still wonder if he wore glasses like his buddy, Willie the Worm.

"TV's are much too expensive," she replied setting meatloaf and potatoes down on the table. "Now go get Kathy, Jim and Jerry in from the backyard. Dinner's ready."

I leaned out the back door and screamed "Get in here, you guys!"

Mom just gave me an exasperated look.

"What?" I asked perfectly innocently.

Several weeks later I was skating home from a strenuous morning of roller skating up at St. Peter's church. (They had the smoothest sidewalks that were great for ball bearing roller skates. Plus, they minimized brush burns on knees.)

All of a sudden, I saw a big van pull up in front of our house. Last time that happened we got a new sofa for the middle room. What? Don't tell me? Yess! I watched in glee as two men gingerly carried an Admiral console TV into OUR house. At last! The Monahan family had finally joined the burgeoning world of TV owners.

That evening, we all sat on the sofa with Mom, hunched forward in anticipation. The boxy brown cabinet before us squawked to life when Dad turned it on and fiddled with the dials. Then, on the rounded-edge square screen, a picture began to take form, with way more than fifty shades of gray, ghostly figures coming to life before our eyes.

We all held our breath. Even baby Jim was captivated as the figures of Kukla, Fran and Ollie morphed into solid shapes.

"Well will ya just look at that!", Dad said in hushed tones normally reserved for church.

A scraggly Beulah Witch popped up then, and joined the happy trio singing 'Here we are, back with you again'. Then, to our delight, Beulah held the stage by herself and sang 'That Old Black Magic' in her raspy, scratchy, 'Bill Tillotson' voice. We were bewitched!

Yes, our family had now joined the masses of Americans that had ditched their console radios for the new kid on the block, *the television set.* I no longer had to trot down the street to Susie's house each afternoon to watch 'Willie the Worm' and 'Western Theatre'. (I am sure her mom was glad to see at least one of those extra kids that crowded into her living room each afternoon finally disappear.)

The dark brown cabinet with the odd shaped screen took up residence in our middle room. We, like many Americans, became familiar with TV models like Philco, RCA, Motorola and our own, Admiral. Almost overnight, television would become an intrinsic part of almost every postwar American's daily life.

But back in the late '40's and early '50's, Americans were new at this TV audience thing. We were only just developing an appetite for entertainment transmitted right into our living room. Our tastes were still quite simple.

Shows like The Lone Ranger, The Ed Sullivan Show, Hopalong Cassidy and Candid Camera were big hits. Westerns and cartoon shows vied with Your Hit Parade, Texaco Star Theater, Your Show of Shows, and The Honeymooners, for our attention. For us kids, The Howdy Doody Show, with its cast of goofballs like Clarabelle the Clown, Phineas T. Bluster and the charming Princess Summerfall Winterspring along with host Buffalo Bob, brought new songs and a host of new phrases into our vocabulary, like 'peanut gallery'.

Now, folks could grab a bag of chips, kick back and become thoroughly engrossed in the little box for hours at a time.

However, it wasn't long before people cultivated an attachment to their favorite TV programs and became more discerning viewers, thereby forcing television producers to 'step up their game'.

With the increasingly insatiable American appetite for better and more varied programming, producers and sponsors figured out where the money was and quickly complied! This created an unholy alliance between art and commerce, or rather TV producers and sponsors.

Television shows swiftly became an instrument for selling the American public things we never even knew we needed. Thus creating the 'commercial interruption to our program', also known in TV land as commercials (or, in our house, as bathroom breaks, snack breaks, check the stove breaks and so forth).

Sponsors realized they had a captive audience, and capitalized on it with gusto! They sold us stuff like soap flakes, toothpaste, cereal, shampoo, cars, Coca Cola, razor blades, cameras, spaghetti sauce and (here's where it gets really Machiavellian), TOYS!

Man, we kids were on cloud nine! Who knew there were such marvelous things, just waiting for Mom and Dad to go and get them for us? Before TV commercials came along, we only had a quick trip to the five and dime or Leh's, Zollinger's and Hess's Brothers Department Stores to scope out the latest arrivals in the toy department.

Now, a plethora of toys presented themselves on a daily basis. Toy trucks, toy cars that you could ride in, toy rifles, dolls that drank water (or Kool Aid if you wanted to experiment), toy ovens and even toy walkie talkies, were ours for the taking. It was a wonderment! Thanks to TV commercials, the world had suddenly become our oyster.

Almost overnight, Americans 'wondered where the yellow went' (Pepsodent toothpaste) and began singing other little ditties like 'Halo is the shampoo that glorifies your hair' and 'Choo Choo Charlie, love my Good & Plentys'. These little gems were designed to keep the consumer singing and *thinking* about a particular product. It's still working today from what I can see!

Another fun and unexpected benefit of those early commercials was that they were shown in real time, 'live' on TV. So, every now and then, something would go disastrously wrong on camera and we got to witness 'in the moment', coffee spilling, tools flying or my personal favorite, Abbe Lane descending a spiral staircase balancing a tray of Coca Cola.

One night, as we watched in 'real time', the gorgeous Abbe (band leader Xavier Cugat's singing eye candy) appeared clad in a tight, slinky gown and was extolling the virtues of Coca cola when she missed a step, and the rest was television commercial history!

But back on Chew Street, our family was just enthralled with the fact that we finally had our very own Admiral TV set.

Heaven had smiled on us, we kids figured. After all, hadn't we all been on our best behavior lately? Not too much whining or fighting going on. No one even got smacked or punched or 'tripped' in days.

Well, there was that one incident with Dad and the hose and the lady and the sidewalk. But, honestly, it was TOTALLY not my fault!

Dad was hosing down the pavement in front of our house. For some unexplained reason, I decided to surprise him and see if he wanted to watch the Willie the Worm show with me.

I slowly crept through the alley from our backyard, carefully avoiding the drainboard that rumbled whenever anyone walked on it.

Carefully peeking out, I watched as he stopped the hose when some people walked by on their way home from the factory down the street.

He had just restarted the hose when *it* happened, kind of like a slow motion movie.

It went something like this.

I peek out and yell, "Hey Daddy, BOO!"

He turns around and yells, "Get back in the yard, Jannie". But as his attention is diverted, his hand slips on the nozzle, the hose flips up just as a lady walks by and…well yeah, it was way worse than Abbe Lane in her slinky dress with Coca Cola sloshing everywhere.
I mean, how was I to know he'd squirt the lady right in the face? Ok, ok, my timing could have been better. A couple of seconds later and he'd have missed her entirely.

But it was so darned funny. To me, anyway.

You know, I never heard him call anyone Madam before. Poor Dad's face was as red as a beet! Anyway, I beat a hasty retreat back through the alleyway and laid low for a couple of hours, completely missing Willie the Worm.

But overall, we kids were well-behaved. So, we naturally assumed we could watch TV anytime we wanted. Wrong! We soon discovered that Mom had other ideas.

Since she was an avid proponent of exercise and fresh air (and just getting *us* out of her hair) lolling around all day watching the Admiral spin his magic web of cartoons laced with a chaser of commercials was definitely not an option. She monitored our TV viewing like a general drunk with the power of his first command!

Since the Admiral lurking in the middle room was new to us, we didn't press our luck, because we knew that now Mom actually had more leverage over us. (This is when we learned strategic withdrawal, or how and when to pick our battles. The troops were not quite ready to revolt.)

Especially after what I called, the 'Ovaltine Affair'. Remember that decoder ring business? Yes well, my friend Cappy neglected to mention that you needed the inside wax cover off a jar of Ovaltine in order to send for the decoder ring, manual and badge. I actually conned Mom into buying a jar of the stuff and happily sent in the cover. I wasn't worried since Captain Midnight assured us on the 'commercial' how great the stuff was.

Well the bloom came off the 'commercial' rose, so to speak, pretty darned quick after I actually tasted the stuff. It was vile! I had to finish the whole jar. But at least I finally got my own decoder ring.

So, we knew we just needed to bide our time and wait for Mom's TV viewing habits to change in order to watch more TV. We figured it wouldn't take too long. But we should have known better because Mom was nothing if not predictable.

For one thing, cleaning had to be done first, then laundry finished and finally dinner prepared, before she would allow herself time to sit down and watch any TV programs.

For a while, the Admiral sat mutely in the middle room, just waiting, waiting for someone to turn it on. Then, one day, Mom finished her house-keeping chores early and decided to watch some TV.

That's when we began our love affair with the actor Jon Hall and his show, 'Ramar of the Jungle'. Along with 'Search for Tomorrow', Ramar became one of Mom's favorite programs. (Frankly I never could understand her fascination for the soap opera, until many years later when I got hooked on 'Dark Shadows'.)

But when we heard that jungle music, the cacophony of laughing birds, the rumble of herds of zebra and saw the lion stalking its prey through the dense jungle vegetation, we were spellbound. Not to mention Jon Hall was a cool looking dude what with that pith helmet and everything!

Dr. Tom Reynolds (Ramar or White Doctor) had a new dilemma each week and we couldn't wait to see what trouble and strife would be in store for him and his sidekick, Professor Ogden. We were captivated.

The Doomed Safari, Flower of Doom, Drums of Doom (can you see a pattern here?) and 'The Curse of the Devil Doll' entranced us all. Of course, I was too young to know that Jon Hall posed an even more dashing figure in his 1937 motion picture with Dorothy Lamour, entitled 'The Hurricane'.

But when we heard those jungle drums, we grabbed our chips, apples and pretzels and dove for a coveted spot on the sofa. I can still see us sitting down to watch 'Ramar', and getting all revved up listening to that exotic jungle music!

What would the good Ramar be up to next? Each week was another exciting adventure and to four kids whose biggest adventure was a trip to River Front Park or the Kift-Mullen Fountain Park down the street, 'Ramar' was the Holy Grail!

For our family and many Americans like us, the dark brown Admiral with the odd shaped screen was the first of what would become a life-long love affair with electronic devices.

But, we never understood the implications of letting the Admiral into our young, innocent lives. Because at the time, this was entertainment, this was news, communication. It was an exciting era of new discoveries and innovations. It was the wave of the future. We were barreling into it!

Who could have ever foreseen that the same vehicle that brought us 'Ramar of the Jungle' and 'Captain Midnight' would, in the not too distant future, bring the first lunar landing right into our living rooms?

Television would take small steps and giant leaps for mankind, becoming a channel of communications the world over. It would teach, entertain, communicate, inform and, horrifyingly enough, one day, it would also show us, in real time, a pair of twin towers collapsing in New York City.

But in 1952, the little Admiral brought delight and joy to our family. For now, we could sit in our living room and be entranced by howler monkeys in jungle tree canopies and laughing birds crying their cuckoo sounds. We could watch spellbound as the king of the jungle prowled through the thick vegetation stalking his prey.

Because, once a week, thanks to the Admiral, we kids could pop onto our sofa and travel into deepest, darkest Africa with the white doctor, '**Ramar of the Jungle'.**

EASTER MEMORIES

In your Easter bonnet,
With all the frills upon it
(Irving Berlin)
Chocolate bunnies, ham and cookies
Rounded out our fun filled day!

I remember the Easter holidays, when we were kids, with a particular fondness. For one thing, Easter, like Christmas, was so indelibly linked to church and family and - food.

Plus, it had its own particular scent! The smell of lilies and hyacinths mingled with the aroma of the fresh baked, rounded loaves of Easter bread called Paska that Mom baked. The bread was a Slovak tradition, handed down through Mom's family from generation to generation. The delicious yeasty aroma permeated the nooks and crannies of our little house on Chew Street. The loaves, filled with raisins and marked with a cross to signify the Holy Day, were placed in baskets with other traditional foods like ham and kielbasa. They would be blessed by the parish priest early Holy Saturday, a custom that my church still observes today.

Just the hint of any one of those aromas now can evoke fond memories of processions at church, of childish hands rummaging through Easter Baskets on Easter morning before Mass, and an Easter Sunday packed to the brim with special foods that blended with the laughter of family and friends.

Easter was, of course, preceded by a most solemn time. In the Catholic Church it was known as Lent. In *our* house it was known as a time of austerity, abstinence and 'Omigod, will Lent ever be over'!

So, the following recollection, dear sister, is how the hustle and bustle of shopping and baking intertwined with the solemnity and somberness of the season that lasted for forty days and forty nights. Mea Culpa!

First of all, the big decision had to be made by Ash Wednesday. My decision went something like this.

"So, Janice, what are you giving up for Lent?"

"Well, I thought I might," I opened my mouth giving a somewhat non-committal reply but my pious friend, Colleen, blathered on.

"I'm giving up chocolate candy *and* ice cream," she went on whilst her halo glowed. I was beginning to feel a bit like Barrabas, since it was almost Ash Wednesday and I hadn't given the matter much thought.

I figured I could always do something unique like recite extra prayers, be especially nice to somebody I really, really didn't like (Colleen), or perhaps kneel on corn for the expiation of my sins. But chocolate *and* ice cream. Just hold on there, chief. Let's think about this for a minute.

Struggling with this choice was always taxing for me. I immediately tossed the 'kneel on corn' thing as too pious. Plus, ow, it hurt! And I didn't think Sister Maria Delecta really meant it when she suggested it. Being nice to somebody I didn't like was fraught with anxiety and doing it for forty days was so not gonna happen! I was a little kid, not a saint!

But, since all the kids at school like Colleen bragged about what *they* were giving up, I kind of got forced into it, if I wanted to preserve my social standing, as it were, as a good Catholic child.

Once the self-denial decision was made, however, another insurmountable object arose to thwart one's holy intentions. How could I even last until Easter Sunday? Forty days was a very long time. Temptation was everywhere.

Temptation number one presented itself early on. Herewith, is a sample.

"How come we're stopping here, Mom?" I asked warily as Dad pulled the car to a halt in front of an unimposing store on Linden Street.

But I already suspected the answer. Because 'here' was the McCandless Wholesale Candy and Tobacco store on Linden Street and we were *not* getting *tobacco*. Not in that big bag Dad returned to the car with. (This was a guy who forbade Mom to empty the ash trays right before payday. He made his ciggies go far. Hey, I'm just saying!)

No, this was our parent's annual trek to buy Easter candy or Easter nests as they were called then, for the four of us.

For the chocolate nest unschooled, this was simply a decorative box of several molded hollow chocolate pieces, like a bunny and some chicks with maybe a little cart or eggs. Included in the large bag, however, was a box of chocolate covered marshmallow bunnies, jelly beans and other assorted Easter delights. I knew this without looking because my chocolate smeller was on high alert. Even though Mom covered the bag pretty well, I sat in the back seat of our car drooling as the devil fanned those chocolate laced vapors my way.

Temptation number two arrived soon thereafter. Herewith, is another sample.

"Jannie, please go next door to Reimer's grocery and get half a pound of butter. Seems we're all out."

"Aw Geez, Mom."

"Now! Jannie."

"I'm going. I'm going!" I stomped all the way to the grocery store.

Now why was *this* a problem? After all, it was only butter! Well the butter was at the back of the store. But the candy counter, tastykakes, ice cream freezer and gum ball machines were right inside the front door.

Gad! Get thee behind me Satan. How could a little kid be expected to cope with *that* kind of temptation? It was downright Machiavellian!

But Mom was Beelzebub's best foil because just when I was succumbing, yielding, beginning to cave, (and searching like an alcoholic on a lost weekend for the bags of chocolate she had hidden), she would gently remind me what time of the year it was and how I only had a little more time to go until Easter Sunday and wouldn't I feel just wonderful then to know I had succeeded in my Lenten abstentions.

One added incentive was that my soul would be beautiful and brilliant! (Once when a nun drew a picture of a soul on the blackboard, it looked like a chalk filled blob to me, so this was not the best argument to sway me.)

Temptations number three through six stalked along through Holy Week. Herewith, yeah, you guessed it!

Because just when we figured the torment was over, Holy Thursday rolled around. This was when the 'being nice to somebody' thing became a real challenge.

Holy Thursday, the first procession of the Triduum. The transfer of the Blessed Sacrament. A somber, solemn church service, cloaked in sacred ritual. Full of holiness, devoutness and godliness. What could possibly go wrong in church? How could the devil and his wiles get me there? Read on!

Preparation for the processions and solemn services began long before Holy Week. For days preceding the big event, we would practice marching around the aisles of Immaculate Conception Church on Ridge Avenue after lunch each day at school. The good sisters weren't taking any chances that we would just show up on Holy Thursday eve in a solemn frame of mind without a few practice sessions first.

In fact, they would assign each of us our places in line and we were paired according to height, so that, two by two, just like Noah's newest best buddies, we would march into church in an orderly fashion in near perfect symmetry.

By the time Holy Thursday arrived, we were pretty much all practiced out and ready to roll, so to speak.

The Sisters of St. Joseph were busy unpacking boxes and boxes of Easter lilies in the church basement. The lilies would be handed to each of us that evening just preceding church services. (After the services, the lilies would be gingerly rewrapped in florists' tissue paper and given back to the nuns for us to use on Holy Saturday.)

All the girls wore white dresses and carried the long-stemmed lilies. Indeed, there was a strict protocol for carrying them. And leave it to the good

St. Joseph's nuns to make sure we knew the proper etiquette for this too. Arms were raised in a cradling position, so that we carried our lilies like precious little white and green babies (ones that smelled really good!).

That Thursday my good friend and line partner Teresa, (a holier girl you never met), and I walked to church dressed in our new white dresses with flower garlands secured in our hair by a ton of bobby pins. Anxious to make sure we got the freshest lilies, Teresa hustled me down the church basement stairs. (I said she was holy but she didn't leave her brains at the door.)

"Did you see Colleen's hair?" Teresa asked as we walked to our places in line. "It looks gorgeous."

"Yeah, I think she got it done at the beauty shop just for tonight," I replied, nervously pushing one of my boingy pin-curls behind my ear. The green-eyed monster was emerging.

We slid into our spots in line as Sister Francine brought us two of the freshest, prettiest Easter lilies. Teresa nudged my arm and smiled the smile of a girl who always knows what she is doing!

I really liked Sister Francine, too. She had the face of an angel and a similar disposition. She made you want to be good. Considering she worked with us kids, day in and day out, this was certainly a stellar achievement.

"Remember, girls, hold them this way," she said gently placing them in our arms.

There was a flurry of activity then as more children poured into the church basement and found their places in line. I watched as Sister Stella followed them down the steps, her black habit billowing behind her. Uh, oh,

Stella was on patrol. And she had her hawk-like eyes and nose fixed on Colleen and Mary Lou.

Then it happened. I watched as Sister Stella slowly and purposefully rolled up the long sleeves of her habit, and then, with astonishing swiftness, she swooped down on Colleen and Mary Lou. Apparently the two of them thought they could switch places with their assigned partners so they could walk together and nobody would notice.

Yeah, right! Anyone in our school with half a brain knew that wasn't gonna happen. Not with Stella on the march.

Sister Stella never missed anything. She had the eyes of a chicken hawk and a nose like one too. Just like the predatory bird, she swooped down on those two chicks, grabbed them by the back of their necks and marched them back to their original places. It was a smooth operation. Mary Lou and Colleen never knew what hit them. I'll just bet the CIA would have loved Sister Stella. She missed her true calling. She could have run a network of spies in Moscow doing dead drops for the CIA.

It was mean, but I couldn't help smiling. Well you know, just because we were in church didn't mean the devil couldn't follow us in. And he did. I think he stood next to me and Teresa when I snickered about Colleen (and her perfect hair). Mea Culpa! And when I snickered again when Sister Stella caught her. But it was hilarious. Mea culpa again!

Suddenly the rumble of the kneelers upstairs told us it was time. The line started to move as we marched up the dimly lit stairs into the church.

"Alright children," Sister Francine whispered. "Remember be prayerful, sing out and careful with the lilies". Her beatific smile sent us on our way.

With the altar arch lights and candles glowing, and chandeliers gleaming, the church was ablaze with the ritual of a centuries old tradition that I was lucky to be a part of. Voices rose to the Sistine chapel-like painted ceiling, as the congregation sang the ancient hymn 'Pange Lingua', penned by St Thomas Aquinas in the 1200's. It was solemn, it was beautiful and it was unforgettable to the little girl that I once was. We filed into our pews at the front of the church, the singing ended and the service began.

Now anyone who ever went to a Catholic school knows that in church the nuns generally sat at the ends of our pews, ostensibly to 'help' us but mostly to keep us from fidgeting (or, God forbid, fighting).

We stood then in our pews as Father McGonigal, garbed in sacred robes, turned and raised the Monstrance, the repository of the Holy Eucharist, aloft. The golden, starburst glittered in the reflection of the altar lights. Jesus was about to be transferred to a place of 'repose' until Holy Saturday. (This was part of the Easter Triduum in the Catholic Church.)

Then several pre-rehearsed things happened at once. Uh, oh yeah, and *one* unrehearsed thing.

Father McGonigle, clasping the Monstrance with his satin stole, slowly, began to descend the altar stairs. As he moved, several men of the parish proceeded to raise the silken canopy under which Father and the altar boys would walk during the procession.

Turning in our pews to face the main aisle, we prepared to file out. Once the singing of 'Pange Lingua' resumed, that was our cue to exit the pew and precede the priest as the procession wound around the aisles of the church.

I should have been in a very holy frame of mind, what with the lily and all. But since the devil was there to distract me, I happened to looked over at the altar as Bucky Egan, an older altar boy and Jimmy Flynn, strode from behind the altar carrying incense burners. He and Jimmy would walk beside Father and swing the censers. Flynn, I might add, was not as adept at swinging the incense burner as Bucky.

Bucky was a heart stopper. Flynn couldn't hold a candle to him (or in this case an incense burner). All the girls in school had a crush on Bucky. Tonight, he looked quite saintly, clad in a white surplice and black soutane. Candle light glistened on his coal black curls and his bright blue eyes shone with a 'religious intensity'. Either that or he was relishing certain events of the previous day.

Because you'd never even guess by looking at him, what with his saintly demeanor and all, that just the day before he had beaten the snot out of Jimmy Flynn for being mean to the new kid, Stefan. (Word on the street had it that Flynn cast aspersions on Stefan's place of origin, Hungary. Bucky was Irish, but he hated intolerance.)

Suddenly I heard Sister Francine gasp. She was looking in horror at Jimmy Flynn and following her gaze I could see that Flynn's size 10's were caught in the front bottom hem of his soutane. With each step he took trying to close the distance to the canopy, his feet became more entangled in the now ripped hem. Smokey incense was pouring from his censer and the hem situation was becoming critical as Flynn wobbled towards the canopy. Flynn's face was red as a beet from his efforts (and probably from the incense too).

Oh, this was too good! In my mind's eye, I could see the canopy bearers going down like ten pins in a bowling alley as Flynn stumbled along. Just when I figured we were about to see some real Holy Smoke, Sister bolted from her place, ran up to the altar and disentangled the flustered Flynn.

Disaster averted! The devil snorted. Father nodded. The bearers exhaled. Sister sighed. Flynn coughed. Bucky smirked. I giggled. And the procession proceeded.

My devout decorum resumed. The clink of the incense burners as they swung back and forth added to the solemnity of the holy ritual. 'Pange Lingua, Gloriosi', our voices resounded. The incense smoke swirled and eddied around our young voices carrying the prayerful notes to the heavens. The solemn procession then wound around the aisles of our church on Ridge Avenue as church goers joined in the singing. The devil was banished, briefly.

Good Friday came and the temptations just kept rolling along. Now old Beelzebub was really ramping it up, because this was when Mom baked her special luscious lekvar squares, drenched in powdered sugar. Of course, when the cookies were done, the raisin infused Paska Easter bread raising on top of the stove, would be ready for the oven. The house smelled like a bakery for days.

Lordy, how would I ever last! But Mom managed to keep all of us kids occupied with small chores even while the devil fanned those sugary lekvar scented sins around our heads. Once the cookies cooled, they were placed in an old silver pretzel can and hidden from prying eyes (and fingers).

Another looming project to keep us busy, was the dyeing of the Easter eggs. After all, what would an Easter Sunday in church be without purple, red and green dyed fingers. So that became a pleasant, if not messy diversion.

But by the time the clock struck twelve noon on Good Friday, all activity came to a halt! Mom was a stickler for preserving the most somber day of the year with appropriate gravity.

For us kids, this was our worst nightmare, and the longest three hours of our young lives. Why? Because we were forbidden to turn on the radio or TV, and the toughest thing of all, we were to remain quiet - I mean *quiet* - positively no talking at all except in dire emergencies (like maybe the house was on fire or the hopper overflowed).

The only reading allowed was our prayer books. (No comics, books or other literature were permitted. This also included coloring books with a purloined crayon or two.)

Three hours of pure silence! This was an aberration! Monahans were never silent, except when they were sleeping, sick, or off to their eternal reward. God, it made me seriously want to rethink the 'kneeling on corn' thing!

So, our Good Friday meditation consisted of reading a prayer book and quietly contemplating the death of Christ on the cross for our sins, past, present and future, while the devil happily wafted cookie, bread and chocolate candy fumes around our goodie deprived heads.

At least all this quiet contemplation put me in a solemn frame of mind for the evening services at church. But quite frankly, I would have preferred a nice nap instead.

Happily, for us kids, though, the approach of Easter also included a secular effect (not counting the candy) that was quite beneficial, especially with all that self-denial, penance and temptation stuff that was going on.

Because this was also the time we shopped for some very special things. Our Easter outfits!

Following a perusal of the Hess Brothers, Zollinger' and Leh's department store ads, we were off to shop. A quick trip on the trolley car uptown, found us in the hustle and bustle of the thriving shopping district of Allentown.

Because, before there were malls, there were tons of stores lining Hamilton Street. Milliners (ladies hats and gloves), dress shops, shoe shops, five and ten cent stores (H.L. Greens, Woolworth's, McCrory's, and Kresge's), purse shops, jewelers, bakeries, candy shops like Schrafft's, the Mohican Market that made pies to die for, restaurants like Betz's Family Restaurant, the Superior, Hess's Famous Patio and the list goes on.

For the girls in the family, this trip meant a new dress, hat, gloves, purse, shoes, and a spring coat. For the boys, suits, shoes, shirts, socks, ties etc. It had to set Mom and Dad back a pretty penny for the four of us. Of course, all these niceties had to last until the following Easter, and God help us if we grew too fast!

Also, on one of these shopping trips into town, we always managed to con Mom into letting us sidle up to the counter at Woolworth's or Kresge's five and ten and watch pastel colored baby chicks huddling together under warm lights.

We always wanted one, and finally one year, Mom actually broke down and bought two, a green one and a blue one. We gave them names and raised them till they got too big for their box and literally had to be farmed out!

We cried when our feathered friends had to depart. They had clearly outgrown their present digs. A chicken coop was out of the question, given the size of our postage stamp yard.

So, we filled their teeny chicken heads with stories of a better life in the sweet country air. A life with lots of room to peck around, good food, glorious sunshine and sweet alfalfa scented breezes. Actually, I was beginning to feel a bit jealous.

In the innocence of youth, we assumed that Archie and Clive would lead idyllic chicken lives with Farmer MacDonald, or in our case Farmer Fenstermaker. It never occurred to us that they might have had a different fate (like meeting up with Colonel Sanders). I console myself now with the fact that Archie and Clive surely must have enjoyed their chicken lives in the pristine country air of Kriedersville, Kutztown or Kuhnsville.

(I didn't know enough about life at the time to understand you should never be on a first name basis with your food.)

Good thing too, because over the years, I have grown to really, really love fried chicken. Uh, as long as I don't know his name.

Holy Saturday arrived and with less than 24 hours to go, it should have been a piece of cake (or candy). But it seemed that was when the devil was at his worst (or best depending on how you look at it).

The day was busy. We spent our time cleaning, helping Mom and getting our clothes out and ready for church. But by the time bedtime rolled around, I was starving for a cookie. So, I did the responsible thing. I drank three glasses of water.

Back in bed, I tossed and turned while my stomach gurgled and sloshed. Giant lekvar cakes, dripping in powdered sugar chased me back and forth, up and down. Why I could almost smell them! I sat up in bed and sniffed. I COULD actually smell them! That's when I noticed the glint of a silver pretzel can peeking out of my wardrobe. Gad. Will the devil never quit? I fell back on my pillow, pulled the covers up over my head and prayed for the swift arrival of morning.

After forty days and forty nights of self-denial, fasting, abstinence, Friday night Stations of the Cross at church, and Friday fish dinners, I pretty much figured out the penitential life of a religious was sooo not for me.

Oh, and guess who HATES fish?

Now what kind of a Supreme Being creates a kid, gives her to CATHOLIC parents and then turns her tastebuds to crap when her mother puts a plate of baked haddock in front of her. One with a bizarre sense of humor, that's who!

But FINALLY, Easter Sunday dawned. All over the city church bells pealed, calling the faithful to worship. Alleluia! Praise Be! Christ is Risen!

In my mind's eye and heart, I can still remember the Easter Sundays of my childhood. They were always sunny and crisp, with just the tease of spring warmth in the air.

Clad in my brand-new Easter outfit, I walked up Ridge Avenue with my family to the red brick, gothic arched edifice that was our church, Immaculate Conception. We entered into a splendiferous scene. Tall lilies, surrounded by fragrant hyacinths, tulips and colorful azaleas, burst forth from the altar like an enchanted spring garden. Candles glowed, chandeliers blazed and the three altar arches radiated with light.

The church was alive with new, green spring life, symbolizing our long dark journey through Lent to be reborn in the promise of Christ on Easter morning. Now we entered into a new season full of promise and renewal. We were re-baptized and God still loved us, despite our imperfections.

Nowhere in the city were there more Alleluias than in the Monahan household. Because now we could FINALLY dive into those Easter baskets, hit up those lekvar squares, and swan around the neighborhood with our friends and cousins in our new Easter outfits.

Now you might be wondering, 'Well, come on, just *what* did she give up for Lent?'

The answer is, EVERYTHING!

Candy, cookies, cake, pies, pastry, ice cream, gum - you name it. See, the way I figured, if I got partway through Lent and say, I gave in and ate a cookie, - well then, I still had all those other goodies to go through before Lent ended.

I may have been holy, but I didn't leave *my* brains at the door either!

RIVERFRONT PARK AND ROMPER DAY MEMORIES

PROLOGUE

For those familiar with the history of the Lehigh Valley, the name 'Trexler' embodies only one person, General Harry Clay Trexler. However, traveling around the valley today, there are reminders of the General everywhere. Some bear his name, others do not. But his legacy looms large, and we citizens of this community are the fortunate recipients of this man's vision and generosity.

General Harry Clay Trexler was a noted business man, philanthropist and community leader in the Lehigh Valley.

Besides running the family lumber business, Trexler was a visionary whose investments in iron, steam heat, electricity, transportation and many other enterprises, made him a very wealthy man. One of those enterprises was the Lehigh Portland Cement Company, which by the late 1920's, was the largest producer of cement in the world. Another was the PPL Company, the area's premier utility company.

Fortunately, for the people of the Lehigh Valley, Trexler was also a generous, community minded gentleman and a great promoter of city planning. He is known as the Father of the Allentown Parks System. But one of his most enduring legacies was the establishment of the Trexler Trust which provided for those parks in perpetuity.

Now some time around the mid 1900's, Trexler was approached by E. L. Manning, Allentown Playground Director and Percy Ruhe, Morning Call newspaper editor and President of the Allentown Playground Association, with the idea of holding a special day of fun and competitions for the city's children.

The General loved children, so the notion of having a fun day of sports and competitions for them appealed to his community spirit. He loved the idea and thus was born "Romper Day". The annual event was to be a day of games, drills, races and competitions celebrating the end of the summer recreation programs held at all of Allentown's playgrounds.

On a bright summer day on August 28, 1914, trolley cars picked up children from the city's nine playgrounds and ferried them to the Allentown Fairgrounds for the first "Romper Day" in the city of Allentown. Over 4000 children participated that day in relay races, calisthenics, drills and, of course, the highlight of the event, the Maypole dance.

Trexler attended Romper Day each year. (It is said that the only time he ever missed a Romper Day was when he journeyed out west to buy bison for the Trexler Game Preserve.)

But back in the 1950's, long after the General had passed into history, I was just a little kid who knew next to nothing about this great man and how much he had done for my community. Nor did I ever give a thought to the gentleman who designed the playground where I had so many adventures with my summertime pals.

This story is remembrance of those summer days long ago.

A Field of Dreams, c1910

Frank Koester squinted into the early morning sunlight. The air held the promise of spring, even though it was only March. The eager civil engineer had only recently embarked on a consulting career in urban planning. He looked over the rough fields – seven acres of them – then turned toward the river. As he walked toward the embankment, a vision began to take shape.

"There," he thought. "Right there."

It was the perfect place for a large, covered pavilion. Overlooking the river below, the pavilion would provide cool shade on hot summer days, catching the breezes off the river. There would also be plenty of room for a boat dock beneath it.

Clutching his rolled up plans, Koester turned around, walked away from the river and began to envision the swings, see-saw's, sliding boards and ball fields in the rough fields all around him.

This plot of land along the Lehigh River was the perfect spot for a playground. He was sure he could design something special for his new client, the city of Allentown. Something for the future children of the city to enjoy for years to come.

In his mind's eye, he could already see children playing on the see-saw while others sailed down the sliding board. Peering into the future, he could hear echoes of their laughter as they soared heavenward on swings and the thwack of a baseball bat hitting one out of the park.

By 1912, following Koester's plans, the city of Allentown created River Front Park along the Lehigh River, turning Koester's vision into a reality.

***

River Front Park, c1950 - Forty Years Later

Squinting into the late morning sun, I watched as one of my flags shot through the air like a guided missile and proceeded to descend rapidly toward Jimmy Flynn's head.

"Serves him right for tripping me this morning," I thought.

Of course, my flag had no business sailing through the air. We were practicing flag drills at the River Front Park Playground and my flag just kind of — took off.

It was a thing of beauty, as it sailed like an arrow right for Flynn's unsuspecting dome. Couldn't have worked out better if I had planned it that way, which I didn't, because then, for sure, I would have missed.

But then my better angels made me yell, "Yo, Flynn. Watch out!" He moved just in time to avert being beaned with my flag and flashed me a dirty look.

"Yo, yourself, Monahan!" he yelled, scowling.

Jerk! I should have just let it fall on his head.

The playground was full of kids that August morning. Some of us were doing flag drills and calisthenics. Later we would practice folk dancing and then, the maypole dance. I liked the folk dancing the best, because I was pretty good at it, unlike flag drills which I obviously was *not*.

I actually did rather well at some of the calisthenics too, but my attempts at the Maypole ribbon weaving was a disaster. Anything that required that much team work and precision was clearly out of my grasp, literally.

Seems I always started out pretty well. Nervously, I would hold my streamer tight as our two circles of kids skipped around the Maypole in time to the lively beat of Old English folk music. Over Billy, under Susie, over Lillian, under Sammy, I whispered to myself. But somewhere along the line, my streamer would get messed up or I would lose count, or drop the streamer and well, team coordination was not my thing. Kind of weird since I was a pretty decent dancer.

When I was a kid, River Front Park Playground was the place to be in the summer. Like all of the playgrounds around the city, it held supervised activities for kids in the surrounding neighborhoods. Besides keeping us all out of trouble, the reason for all this frenetic activity was our preparation for "Romper Day".

"Romper Day" was *the* annual event held at the Allentown Fairgrounds where children celebrated the end of the playground summer recreation program with relay races, dances and other sports events.

The day of fun and games included a free lunch, along with prizes. Named Romper Day for the white rompers the children once wore, most kids now, in the 1950's, wore white shorts and shirts for the big day. Some even had their playground colors added to their outfits.

On this particular summer morning, we had been practicing our hearts out in preparation for the end of summer annual blast.

When the drill was over, we put away our flags and proceeded to practice our folk dancing. The morning flew by as we jumped, skipped, raced and then finally, danced around the Maypole.

Later, after a morning of physical activity that would daunt an Olympic athlete, my friend Teri and I sat on the swings. Twisting our swings around in a dreamy fashion, we began to discuss the upcoming 'event.'

The August sun beat down on our heads and I dug my buster brown sandals into the gravelly dirt beneath my swing, twisting and then twirling my swing in dizzying circles. All organized activities were over for the morning, and most of our playground pals had gone home and onto other pursuits, like lunch.

"So, Jan, do you think your Mom will let you go next week?"

"I dunno," I replied, a bit downcast. "You know how she is about letting me go places without her."

"But our playground instructor will be there with lots of other chaperons," Teri pointed out.

"Oh, I know. But every time I ask about going, she says she doesn't want me running amok at the fairgrounds with all those kids."

Personally, the "running amok" part sounded like a pretty good deal to me. But this was one of those times when having a cop for a dad was definitely a disadvantage.

He saw so many bad things happening to kids, it was a wonder he and Mom had even let me come down to River Front Park without either of them. But I guess Mom figured that Teri and I would be together, so there was safety in numbers.

"Rats," Teri sighed. "We could have a great time. There's even a free lunch."

"Yeah, I know. I heard that last year everyone got a hot dog, a drink and an orange creamsicle, too," I said, scraping my shoes into the gravel again.

I knew Mom would make me polish my shoes when I got home, but I didn't care. So what! The more Teri and I talked about Romper Day, the more irritated I became.

It wasn't just missing the free hot dog lunch that had me miffed, but losing out on the whole Romper Day experience was really ticking me off.

Romper Day was a big deal because you got to ride on a trolley car and travel way out to the west end of the city. The huge extravaganza was held at the Allentown Fairgrounds and kids from playgrounds all over the city would be there, participating in drills, relay races, dancing and singing.

Back then, I was just a little girl who wanted to be with her pals. Yeah, even Flynn.

I was beginning to rail against parental control.

Teri and I began the long, hot, two block walk home with me grousing all the way about not being allowed to go to "Romper Day".

I slogged through my kitchen door with the weight of the world (and Romper Day) on my slender eight year old shoulders, slid into my chair at the table and sighed. Several times. Loudly.

Finally I asked, "What's for lunch, Mom?"

"How about a sandwich? Lebanon bologna ok?"

"Yeah, uh yes," I replied.

Mom slid the sandwich in front of me and I bit into the spicy-sweet bologna sandwich I loved. The white Freihofer's bread was super fresh, just the way I liked it. Lebanon bologna on super fresh white bread is to die for, a Pennsylvania Dutch delicacy as far as I'm concerned.

After I polished off half of my sandwich, I began to notice Mom seemed upset about something.

Well, it couldn't have been me. Hey, I was at the playground all morning, so it wasn't anything I did. My two other siblings were already napping, so they were in the clear. Baby Jimmy was in his high-chair squashing a banana between his chubby fingers, so he was probably out of the running.

That's when I noticed the newspaper opened on the edge of the table.

Now being the whip smart Sherlock of clues that I was, I figured she saw something in the paper that wasn't good. Yeah, well. "What else is new," I thought.

But then I began to wonder. What *did* Mom read in the paper this time? What kid disappeared, was kidnapped, drowned in the river, got hit by a car or — well, name your poison.

I was also smart enough to figure out that this was going to have a direct impact on my attendance at Romper Day. (If Mom was a worry-wart, Dad was even worse. It was a no-win situation, from my perspective.)

But hope springs eternal. I began to think that maybe they would change their minds. Why not? That could happen. In my lunchtime fantasy, they would say, *together of course*, "Well certainly you can go, dear. It will be lots of fun for you. What a wonderful learning experience. Have a good time."

Um, yeah right, *in my fantasy.*

I glanced over at my baby brother in his high chair as he tried to eat some more chunks of banana. The kid didn't have a care in the world. He looked up at me and gave me a semi-toothless grin. Bet *he'd* never have a problem going to Romper day.

"Jannie, please take Jimmy out in his stroller for a bit after lunch," Mom said as she tidied the kitchen.

"Sure," I replied. "Hey Jimbo, wanna go for a ride?"

He started kicking his legs and squirming in his high chair. Guess that's a yes. Sheesh. The kid already knew the 'ride' word.

Ok, well, the sooner he was ready for a nap, the sooner I could go back out and play with my pals, where we could devise a plan and discuss ways to con my Mom and Dad into letting me go to Romper Day.

Although, glancing at James wiggling in his high chair, the little darling didn't look very sleepy to me.

Drat!

This was going to take work! And that meant that I would probably be pushing him up and down Chew Street until *I* needed a nap.

Double Drat.

Mom took the stroller out to the front sidewalk and put James in it.

"Stay where I can see you, Jannie," she instructed. "Don't go any further than Ridge Avenue. Just turn around and come back and no crossing busy streets."

"Ok, Mom. Don't worry," I said giving the scratched and dented stroller a push.

Once, in a former life, the tin stroller had been blue with cream trim and had a wooden push handle. The front tray had wooden beads that spun around, supposedly to keep baby occupied during a stroll. But after four kids, it was literally on its last legs, er, rollers. Squeaky, with no padding and a foot tray that fell apart every fifty feet, the thing was a rolling death trap.

"And don't go too fast," Mom called after me, as I squeaked up the block. Funny what moms find to worry about.

"I won't," I replied. My words hung in the hot August air, as I sailed past my friend Helen's house.

It was a quiet afternoon in the neighborhood. Nobody seemed to be around as I pushed the stroller past red brick row homes and teeny side yards. I started to hum lullabies thinking maybe that would make James sleepy. Instead *I* started to yawn, while James kicked his feet and wiggled and chatted to himself. Nope. So much for that idea.

On our fifth tour up and down Chew Street, I looked down at my little passenger. He was enjoying the ride and *sooo* not sleepy. But, brother, I sure was getting tired of pushing the stroller *and* singing lullabies. My legs felt like rubber and I was getting seriously thirsty after scarfing down my Lebanon bologna sandwich.

I kept on humming "rock-a-bye baby" while I thought about how I could convince Mom to loosen the parental reins and let me go to Romper Day.

I needed a plan or a convincing argument. I had neither. Zip. Nada.

Pretty soon I noticed my passenger starting to nod off. Yesss! We scooted and squeaked for home.

As I pushed the rickety stroller with my semi-comatose passenger into the back yard, I could hear Mom talking to someone on the phone.

"Yes, I read it in the paper just this morning. Imagine, hit by a car that was trying to pass a trolley, and at the Fairgrounds of all places. Poor child," Mom said into the receiver, her voice filled with gloom and despair.

Holy Cow! That's all I had to hear. I knew it! My Romper Day trip was doomed.

My grand plan and convincing argument was just torpedoed by the very trolley car I wanted to ride on.

Man, I could already see all my playground pals boarding a trolley car bound for the west end of Allentown as I tearfully waved farewell.

Farewell, pals. Farewell Romper Day. Farewell Susie, farewell Sammy. Yeah, and farewell Flynn, too.

Triple Drat!

***

It had been a week since Romper Day. Teri and I didn't talk much about me missing it and I wasn't mad anymore – just resigned. Gradually, I came to understand that the best prize of all was just playing with my pals at River Front Park all summer.

The two of us watched from the Pavilion at River Front Park as the little pedestrian ferry with a flat roof and benches chugged across the river towards Adams Island. We stood on the bottom of the railing, leaning over and waving to the few passengers, while sunlight sparkled on the waves churned up by the ferry.

As we leaned on the railing, we could smell the fishy scent of the river mingled with the ever present yeasty scent of Neuweiler's brewery next to the playground.

We slurped orange creamsicles, the creamy vanilla ice cream on a stick dipped in orange sherbet, its sticky coldness dripping on our fingers.

"Someday, I wanna ride on that boat," I announced.

"Yeah, me too. Although it does go kind of slow," she observed.

"Bet it would be fun, though," I replied wistfully. "Except, I really don't know anybody over there."

"Me neither," Teri replied biting a chunk of her creamsicle.

"Over there" was Adams Island, a tiny chunk of land across the river from River Front Park. Just a spit of land, really. It was dense with trees and populated with colorful cottages that hugged the edge of the river.

However, for two little eight-year old girls who had never set foot upon it, the place held its own mystery. It could have been inhabited by wild animals for all we knew or whatever else our imaginations could conjure.

We watched as the ferry plied its way slowly across the river, chug chugging against the current. Finally, it docked on the other side of the river, and began to discharge its few passengers who disappeared into their cottages and backyards.

Then the ferry's motor rumbled, churning up more waves and the little boat proceeded to begin its return trip. A few more passengers had ambled down to the small loading dock.

We watched silently, still slurping our melting creamsicles, as the ferry chugged and rumbled.

For now, Romper Day with all its attendant hoopla and hype was over and pretty much forgotten as far as I was concerned.

Did I ever get to attend a Romper Day? No, not really. And it would not be the last time   I missed an event because my parents couldn't guarantee my safety.

But my eight-year old self couldn't comprehend that having a policeman for a dad wasn't just about him riding around in a snazzy squad car or wearing a cool looking uniform and a gold shield on his hat brim.

No, there was much more to his job than that. More than I knew.

Because, as a police officer, Dad *did* have to deal with the results of a child getting hit by a car. He *did* witness the outcome of a child drowning. He *was* there in front of a parent when a child went missing. Over the course of his years on the force, he *was* present too, at many other tragedies involving children and their families. None of which he ever discussed in my or my siblings' presence.

In addition to being an excellent cop and Dad, he did all he could to preserve our innocence from the harsher realities of life.

My non-attendance at Romper Day had now become a distant memory. Summer was winding down and fall was on our doorstep. I had other things to think about.

Soon we would be returning to school. With the nimble minds of the very young, Teri and I turned our attention to that very same pressing matter.

"Wonder if we're going to have Sister Mary Claire this year," Teri said.

"I hope so. I heard she's really nice. She hardly ever yells," I replied. I always hated teachers who yelled all the time. Scared the daylights out of me. Which was, I guess, the whole point.

With the ferry and Adams Island forgotten, Teri and I chattered then like magpies about going to the fifth grade. Cool breezes off the river ruffled our hair.

"Did you get any dresses yet?" I asked.

"No, not yet, but I'm getting a new school bag this year," she confided. "My old one was my sister's but my mom promised to buy me my own."

"They had some neat plaid ones at Woolworth's," I told her. "You know, down in the basement part of the store." You could find just about anything at Woolworth's.

"My mom said she'd get me a new pencil box and some Marble copy books," I continued. I always liked that the copy books had the times tables on the back. In case you got stuck in arithmetic and couldn't remember eight times four, Mr. Marble copy book was a Godsend.

But Teri was pretty darned good at arithmetic. She had helped me out on a few occasions. I learned early on, if you want to look smart, hang out with smart people.

School bags and copy books decided, our conversation took yet another turn.

"Hey, I learned some new steps in ballet class. Wanna see?"

"Yeah, show me." Teri stood by my side.

Demonstrating my balletic prowess, I leaped into the air, my skinny arms stretched out before me, one hand still clutching my slowly melting creamsicle.

"Hey, that's neat. I can do that too," she said following my lead and leaping into the air beside me.

As passersby watched and smiled at our antics, two eight-year old girls, with not a care in the world, danced and twirled, leaped with abandon, their laughter and giggles filling the pavilion while they tried to outdo one another's dance steps.

The delighted echoes of our laughter rose into the air, just like the joyous cries of hundreds, perhaps thousands of children who had enjoyed River Front Park before we two were born.

Briefly that golden childhood moment lingered, echoing under the pavilion. But even for two little girls, time did not stand still that day. That moment in time slipped away. Vanishing like vapors into the air. Like children everywhere, we didn't appreciate then how precious were those innocent moments of joyous abandon.

The afternoon sun lowered in the sky. It was getting late. Soon it would be time to head home for supper. Our idyll at the park was almost over.

"Hey, Jan, wanna do the swings before we have to go home?" Teri asked flipping her popsicle stick in the trash can.

"Race ya," I yelled and we took off at a dash for our favorite swings.

***

Author's Note:

In 1973 River Front Park was renamed for another great Allentonian, George 'Bucky' Boyle. Mr. Boyle was a sports legend and outstanding baseball player who founded Allentown's Downtown Youth Center in 1947. He was a champion of youth sports and was dedicated to young people.

The people of the Lehigh Valley have been extremely fortunate that men like General Harry Clay Trexler and George 'Bucky' Boyle gave so much to their community.

Their legacies live on in the laughter and joyful cries of the thousands of children who continue to enjoy the playgrounds and parks of Allentown and Lehigh County.

As for Romper Day, the tradition continues to this day under a more modern title. Now called Playground Celebration Day, it has entertained and delighted the children of Allentown for over 150 years.

I do not know if city planner Frank Koester ever really visited the city, although I am sure he must have come to the area at some point, since his clients included Allentown, Bethlehem and Scranton.

I like to think that he *did* walk those rough fields. Now, after all these years, the park he designed continues to serve its community and a beautiful pavilion still catches the breezes off the Lehigh River and overlooks Adams Island.

More importantly, I do find it interesting, and an odd coincidence, to note that the first Romper Day was held on August 28th, Frank Koester's birthday. Perhaps General Trexler managed that too!

MOVING DAY!!

We're movin' on up,
To the west end,
To a deeluxe ranch,
In Hamilton Park!

We bought a new house! It was in the west end of the city where rich people lived, at the other end of town. It had a blue tiled bathroom, living room and dining room and three neat bedrooms, with closets. It had a modern kitchen with a new white gas stove and white cabinets. (We chose to overlook the fact that the kitchen was not much bigger than a closet.)

The outside of this miniscule mansion was clad in white shingles and black shutters. Two big picture windows overlooked South Street, which was at present still to be paved. (Torrents of rain had produced gullies a small car could get lost in.) Since no one lived at this lower end of South Street yet, I guess the city fathers figured they didn't need to pave it. That was about to change.

The house had a huge basement with nothing in it except a small gas furnace which was nothing like our coal burning, ash belching monster on Chew Street. There was no sulfurous smelling coal bin either, no need for one. The basement was light and airy and had plenty of room for Mom's washer and (more importantly) our toys. It smelled like newly poured concrete and dust.

Best of all, our new house had a **huge** backyard with *no* fence.

We were so excited. We were actually moving, leaving the 'ward', relocating to the west end, going to a new school, moving across 'the tracks'.

Post war America was looking towards the suburbs for a better life for their families away from crowded inner cities and crime and we were no exception. (Although if there was any crime in our neighborhood on Chew Street, I never heard of it, except maybe the occasional broken window.)

But I'm sure Dad was thinking of the future. He could see the shift in the population and the progression toward the suburbs. Anyway, we would not be playing dodge ball in the city streets or alleys or jumping around the loading docks at the cigar factory on Front Street anymore. The air was a lot cleaner in the suburbs with less traffic. Not like our neighborhood on Chew Street with constant truck traffic and the meat packing plant and brewery a scant two blocks away in either direction.

I was probably about ten years old when we moved, because that's when I started the sixth grade at St. Catherine of Sienna School. I am sure I told my friends on Chew Street we were moving, but it didn't register that I would not see them anymore. (At least, not for a few years until I started Central Catholic High School.)

I honestly don't remember feeling bad about leaving my friends and I don't remember even saying a big sloppy goodbye to them. There was too much excitement going on about moving.

We had been in a tizzy for weeks. Boxes we had been packing for weeks were stacked in the front room of our little row home and we had already been to see 'our new house', further fueling our anticipation.

The white shingled ranch style house was brand new. No one had ever lived in it before. (Probably because it stood vacant for over a year waiting for just the right suckers - er, family to buy it.) It still had that new house smell.

The backyard was humongous by Chew Street standards. Of course, it needed a little work, like a lawn, a walkway and a patio with flowers and shrubs, but all that would come later.

Eventually Mom and Dad would repaint all the woodwork a crisp shiny white and every room would be wallpapered. There would be frilly white Priscilla curtains on all the windows and new carpeting to cover the hardwood floors. My sister and I would get two new twin Hollywood beds with green headboards trimmed with brass nail heads.

For now, though, school was out for the summer, and we packed and cleaned frenetically, inching towards the big day. Finally, moving day arrived. Of course, since it was July in the city, it was another hot, sticky and overcast summer day.

Plans had been made and Mom had all the boxes and furniture organized. In our never-ending quest to save money, we did not rent a moving van. That was for rich people. No, instead, Dad knew a guy who knew a guy who knew somebody who had a truck we could use.

Dad's buddies showed up bright and early with the pick-up truck. At least, I think it was a truck. It wheezed up to the curb and let out a sigh. This was before we loaded it. Mom took one look at the wreck and her face fell.

Not only was it on its last legs, but the tiny truck bed wouldn't hold much of our stuff. Obviously, it was going to take numerous trips across town until all our belongings were moved.

Not to worry, though. We kids were there to help!

We watched in fascination as the guys loaded as much of our belongings into the truck bed as they could (legally). The stuff in the truck kept getting higher and higher as we handed the guys boxes and bags. By the time they said 'enough', the loaded truck looked like something out of the 'Grapes of Wrath' movie with chairs sticking out, mattresses standing tall against the sides of the truck bed and boxes wedged in at odd angles.

Dad hopped in and started the truck. The motor wheezed and coughed to a rumbling 'chuk itta chuk', a steady, if not promising purr of the motor.

But behind the purr came another far off rumbling noise. Please God, let it not be. But it was. With a crack like a whiplash, thunder rumbled down Ridge Avenue, made a left turn and rolled right down to our doorstep on Chew Street.

Before you could say, "Holy Cow! This truck doesn't have a roof," the heavens opened up and dumped on our just loaded mattresses!

A mad scramble ensued to find some kind of covering for all of our things. A couple of shower curtains later, we waited under the eaves for the downpour to stop. Poor Mom was beside herself. It seemed we had planned for everything but the weather. Of course, knowing our luck, it probably wouldn't have mattered anyway. Plus, it was probably the only time Dad could get his buddies and the truck together at the same time.

Finally, the rain let up, the truck rolled off and we proceeded to get ready for the next load.

Soon, Dad and his buddies returned and we loaded up again. The piles in the house were getting lower, but it was pretty evident two trips weren't going to cut it. After a bit of hemming and hawing, the truck was as full as it was going to get. The guys jumped in, Dad turned on the ignition, a cough, a rumble, a sigh, a 'chuck itta chuck' and then, out of nowhere, a terrific 'Boom'. It was *not* the truck.

You guessed it. Thunder rolled in again. As sure as Noah said, "Why me, God?" the heavens opened up into a torrential downpour.

So, this was pretty much the way the rest of the move went that day. Poor Mom tried to do her best, but there was no stopping the weather. It was as though Chew Street could not bear to see us leave and the heavens were sorely miffed at our imminent departure. In the meantime, we kids ran in and out of the rain looking like drowned rats.

At long last the little row house on Chew Street was empty and we all piled into our car, slightly damp but still elated. The Reimers' and the Steiners' and a whole bunch of other neighbors came out to see us off as we bid them and the old neighborhood a fond farewell!

But with the ignorance of youth, I never realized that we were leaving behind some of the best people in the world. That there were some friends I would never see again. Nor did I comprehend that Chew Street would never be the same or look the same again for anyone. It seemed with our departure, the old neighborhood had changed forever in the blink of an eye.

We were moving to the suburbs. But what I didn't understand was that this was a big trade off. Yes, we would have a lovely, though small, suburban home with a big yard. But there was no drug store only a block away where I could go for an ice cream sundae. There was no hairdresser living right across the street like my hair dresser Pauline. There was no school or church within walking distance. Nor was there a grocery store like the Reimer's only steps away where I could pop over and buy penny candy anytime I had a spare penny.

We would be living in the suburbs, a strictly residential area. Things like stores, churches, schools, beauty parlors, all required a car or bus to reach. One visited with neighbors only if one was invited. There would be no sitting on the front porch at nights and chatting. There would be no calling over back yard fences as you hung out the wash.

We were going to the suburbs. Overnight, it seemed, our lifestyle had changed drastically.

In time, we would learn, absorb and acquire the many skills our suburban culture dictated. For instance, our new friends would not always live right down the street. Also, we would need to let Mom know just exactly where we were going to play. (Our borders were within one block of her sightline. A slight hindrance if our new friends lived two blocks away.) And don't even think of skipping four blocks down to Union Terrace Park without adult supervision. (Mom didn't have to worry about us drowning in the Lehigh River anymore. No, now she worried about us drowning in the lake at Union Terrace.) We had more space alright, but now we also had more rules.

Welcome to the suburbs. There was a reason people were spread out and not on top of their neighbors. They wanted it that way!

Eventually, we would play in our big yard, build tree forts, chase rabbits on a summer's night, sled down our embankment on a snowy day, but we would never again live in a close-knit neighborhood where people looked out for one another like they did on Chew Street.

Now, across town in the suburbs, a little ranch house on Leh Street awaited its new family with damp mattresses and lives sealed in cardboard boxes. It was a house that had yet to become a home. Fresh paint, shrubs, furniture and flowers were still in its future and our imprint on the modest ranch was yet to be. That would all take time.

This then was our future. But with the obliviousness of youth, I took very little time saying goodbye to the past.

Now, with the wisdom that only hindsight can bring, I wished I had taken a last look at that teeny back yard where my three-year old self pushed down the fence rungs as I climbed on them day after day and where cousin Denny and I made mud pies when were tots. I should have climbed up to the attic to watch the dust motes settling, reminding me of all the times I would sneak up there to get a peek at my Christmas presents. I would have taken a last look at my little bedroom with the blue sprigged flower wallpaper (which in a moment of three-year old artistic abandon I had decorated with Mom's red lipstick.) A last trip to the spotlessly clean old basement with whitewashed walls where Mom had bathed all four of her babies would have been next.

Had I known then how much it would really matter to me someday, I would have looked once more around the kitchen where we played ping pong with our vegetables, where Uncle Joe teased Jerry about pronouncing 'masshhed' potatoes and where you, dear sister, managed to pull down a steel base cabinet on yourself escaping injury like Houdini himself.

I would have taken a peek at the corner in the middle room where you bounced so hard in your playpen that you flipped it over and ended up penned like a caged critter!

Once more, I would have strolled down Chew Street, where I used to walk baby Jimmy in his stroller that broke down every five feet. I would have looked long and hard at the pavement in front of our little house where my good friends Teresa or Dolly or Helen and I played hopscotch, jump rope or just sat on the stoop playing jacks. Finally, I would have slipped noiselessly through the long alleyway between our house and Steiner's all the while remembering the countless furtive sneaks in and out of our backyard.

Every room in the little row home was packed to the brim with thousands of happy, loving memories. It was chock full of remembrances of a young, growing family just starting their journey in life. A family that started with three and grew to six souls, connected forever.

Memories of Baptisms, Christmas trees, Easter eggs, the first day of school, the first bike, the first roller skates, the first television (with Willie the Worm and Uncle Miltie), filled each and every nook and cranny. The ever-changing parade of our cars parked in front of our house over the years, each one a little bit better than the last, witnessed our progress as we moved on up.

By working so hard to create a home, our parents had given us so much more. They never had much money, but we never ever felt poor or deprived. We lived in a good neighborhood surrounded by love and all the comforts they could provide their four children. Their sacrifices gave us a happy, secure family life.

If houses could sing, the walls of our row home on Chew Street would have reverberated with our songs, our laughter, our tears and our voices filling its rooms to the attic rafters. It had protected us, sheltered us and kept us safe for over seven years.

It simply would not do to break faith with the little house now. We cleaned and polished our loyal friend inside and out while it waited staunchly for its new life.

In true Monahan family fashion, Mom and Dad sold the house to another young family just starting out.

Now, it would be their turn to make memories!

THE CHESTNUT INN

Sometime in the 1700's, Chief Tallee of the Lenni Lennape Indians, like his forebears, took his family to their summer retreat on an island along the Atlantic coast.

The surrounding marshes were plentiful with birds and shell fish. Tallee also recognized the benefits of the sun and salt sea air on his family. Also, he knew the fishing was great and the loamy, sandy soil was good for certain crops.

The tribe could eat like kings for the summer months. It was a natural wonder, and Tallee and his family pretty much had the place to themselves. On cool summer evenings they would sit by their cook fires and listen to the waves break on the shore.

Sadly, for Tallee and his tribe, a few years later, Jeremiah Leeds found the place, and built the first permanent structure there. It wasn't too long before more structures popped up, which became the Leeds Plantation, firmly planting the first white man in the area.

Years later, Doctor Jonathan Pitney discovered the island and immediately realized the healing properties of a stay along the shore on Absecon Island. What a great health resort it would make, he surmised! Pitney knew others would also love it and began to think about how to get people to and from the island.

Happily, for Pitney, in 1854, the railroad cometh. And so did tourists.

Hotels and businesses quickly blossomed to accommodate the gaggles of tourists. In the 1870's, a boardwalk was built to help tourists keep from tracking sand into pristine hotel lobbies.

No longer would the nomadic Tallee and his family make their annual trek to their place by the sea. They were long gone.

Instead, the beautiful beach with the rolling surf lured thousands of tourists and became known as Atlantic City.

In 1953, it became the Monahan family's turn to discover this place by the sea. With all due respect and apologies to Tallee and the Lenni Lennape, our resemblance to a band of nomadic Indians was purely coincidental.

***

Before there was Expedia.com and other travel research wizards, one depended upon either the kindness of friends to recommend vacation accommodations, or snazzy, colorful brochures that showed azure skies, pristine pools and sumptuous rooms. Of course, one other option was the tried but not always true method, "Pull over here, dear, that looks like a nice place!"

So, as it happened, on one such Monahan family vacation, we had occasion to use at least one of these methods. We can pretty much rule out the brochure thingy here, and the pull over method never worked out for us, which leaves us with the friend's recommendation (or in our case, the friend of a friend).

Vacations and road trips with our family were always an unforgettable experience. For one thing, they were highly memorable because they were few and far between, cost being an important factor. While some of our trips were more notable than others for various reasons, I do remember a particularly interesting trip we once took to Atlantic City.

Excitement ran high when we learned we were going to Atlantic City. Are you kidding me? Going anywhere was cause for immediate and prolonged celebration. We were buzzed. A real vacation was imminent. I could almost smell the fudge and salt water taffy!

Bumping into one another, we tore through our dressers looking for swimsuits, shorts, sneakers and the like. We needed to pack all of our stuff, and help load up the car.

On my third trip out to the car I began to worry a bit though, because only two weeks before, our latest car, a 1947 Pontiac streamliner, broke down and had to be given a push after a picnic at the Police Home. (If there were twenty cars on a lot and only one was a lemon, it would find Dad.)

It was a cool looking car though, if you can call the fastback streamliner with a visor, fender skirts and a once pale green paint job that now looked like cement dust, cool.

But the prospects of a road trip and vacation in Atlantic City beckoned, and diminished any worries I had of being stranded along the road somewhere.

Finally, the car trunk was loaded with suitcases, beach toys and snacks and we were off.

Back in those days, a trip to Atlantic City, New Jersey from our house in Pennsylvania was a tedious affair, as we navigated back roads through one small town after another. So, being trapped in the car with four whiny kids for hours, surely tried Mom and Dad's patience. Although, in our own defense, I have to say they were lucky because at least none of us ever got carsick.

The trip started out well enough because we were all on our very best behavior. In fact, we were nauseatingly nice to one another, even considerate

— in the beginning. But after being squashed into the back of the Pontiac for hours on end, the novelty of the trip gradually wore off and boredom set in. That's when "stuff" began to happen.

Let's say, for the sake of argument, one of us committed a grievous offense, such as invading the other's space (and in our old car, this was not hard to do). Inevitably, THE warning came from Dad.

You know, the old "Don't make me stop this car or you *will* regret it" threat! Shrewdly, we never made him "stop this car." We were rambunctious, not stupid!

Peace reigned for a time in which we played games or told knock-knock jokes. But then we became silly and giddy and LOUD which was even worse than smacking each other around. Then a fine whine would emanate from the back seat (and I'm not talking Pinot Noir here).

After the tenth "Are we there yet?" it must have been like Dante's seven rings of punishment for Mom and Dad just to be in the car with us!

But by the time we *finally* got close to 'the shore' as it was then known in better vacation circles, the smell of the marshes and the approaching Atlantic City skyline curtailed our squabbling. Model behavior resumed.

Yes! We had finally reached our destination. Our excitement level rose palpably. Miraculously, the chattering and bickering ceased, being replaced by an awesome quiet.

Smelling that briny salt sea air, and seeing glimpses of the boardwalk skyline meant we were almost there! (It also meant lunch.)

As the Pontiac tooled into the city that day in 1953, passing luxury hotels and fine restaurants, soft murmurs of "There's a nice hotel. Is that where we're staying?" and "Mom, can we stop at that restaurant?" were uttered by various occupants of the back seat. Response one from Mom, "No", to the hotel and "Definitely not," to the restaurant. Response two from Dad, "I am not a banker!"

However, we were so engrossed in opulent looking hotels and toney restaurants, we didn't notice our detour down a rather unimposing street.

The Pontiac pulled up in front of a squarish, three-story red brick building. Gazing up at the brick façade, I was immediately reminded of something I had seen before, but I couldn't quite remember what it was.

There were several steps up to a wide porch as I recall. I suppose it was designed to be imposing but it just missed the mark. The black and white sign out front read "The Chestnut Inn".

"What is *this place*?" Jerry whispered, looking up at the grim looking building.

Well he might wonder about *this place*. Because, walking up the steps, I suddenly realized why it looked so familiar. It was a dead ringer for the County Juvenile Detention Center. (No, I was never incarcerated there. But similar to "the poor starving children of Africa" axiom, the possibility of visiting the place was often used as a deterrent by Dad.)

However, at the time, no one but me seemed to notice the similarity to houses of detention. After all, it *was* a hotel, recommended by a friend of a friend, even.

So, Dad checked us in and off we went to our rooms. The boys were to bunk in with Mom and Dad, and thinking they were doing us a favor, the folks got our very own room for you and me, dear sister, across the hall.

The room seemed nice, with a double bed, a dresser, two night stands, a chair and two blue plaid curtained windows that overlooked the street. Since we hadn't stayed at too many hotels, we didn't have anything else with which to compare it. Besides, we were actually in a hotel, in our very own room! Opening drawers and closet doors, we proceeded to check out the room and then gave the bathroom a once over.

Cool! White subway tile, light and clean, lots of fluffy towels and soap in little wrappers too, and a bathtub big enough to swim laps in. It was huge compared to ours at home. We promised ourselves a luxurious bath that night. We could run tons of water, and nobody would yell at us.

Since we had arrived later than planned due to our circuitous route, the game plan for the day (in our family there was always a game plan, rather like the D-Day invasion) was to take a lovely stroll on the boardwalk, get lunch and then we would hit the beach.

Taking barely anytime to unpack, we were off to the boardwalk. As I skipped up the side street, I could see the ramps leading up to the boardwalk in front of me, already filled with a steady stream of tourists coming and going.

I ran up the ramp to the boardwalk and crossed to the railing where I could look down at the beach — and the ocean. A muffled roar mingled with the sounds of people laughing, people talking and people just having fun greeted me. After driving through the traffic filled streets of Atlantic City, suddenly seeing that broad expanse of water was just awesome.

Sunlight glistened on rolling waves, and the roar of the surf slapping the shore muted the sound of happy beach goers. We listened spellbound as the shrieking of seagulls mingled with the squeals of delighted children feeling the cold waves on their toes.

The wide beach was filled with people, beach blankets and colorful umbrellas, dotting the sandy stretch. Children ran back and forth to the water, shouting and laughing. A scent of sun tan oils, popcorn and salt sea air rolled up to greet us. It was an amazing sight, or so we thought.

Until we looked southward, and saw IT!

"IT" was "The World Famous Steel Pier." The massive man-made pier, half a mile long, jutted out into the great green ocean. Known as the Playground of the World, The Showplace of the Nation and other superlatives, it was an awesome sight to four little kids from Pennsylvania.

Back in those days, the Steel Pier was known for its exciting array of entertainment. Acts like Rex the Wonder Dog, Boxing Kangaroos, and of course, those marvelous, *death defying* "diving horses", entertained thousands of visitors year after year.

We didn't know it at the time, but in 1931, a young woman named Sonora Carver lost her sight when her horse lost his balance on the diving platform and plunged forty feet into the twelve foot pool below. Sonora was blinded when she hit the water with her eyes open. But Sonora kept on diving for eighteen years, eleven of them blind, until 1942. Many years after we visited Atlantic City, Sonora's story inspired the movie "Wild Hearts Can't Be Broken". To this day, I wished I could have seen the spectacle of a horse and rider diving forty feet into that pool.

The pier also hosted shows by George Hamid featuring the most talented artists of the day, like Frank Sinatra and a current teenage heart throb, by the name of Bobby Rydell.

On this day in 1953, the Steel Pier hummed with activity. Halfway out on the pier, a huge Ferris wheel dominated the skyline. From where we stood, it seemed suspended in the hazy, summer sky.

"Hey, Dad, can we go there?" Jimmy asked, his eyes widening at the sight.

"Maybe later," Dad replied. This was Dad speak for, probably not. He could probably hear the ca-ching of cash registers as the four of us ran around savoring the delights of the pier.

It *was* an astounding sight, and like any fairyland, we didn't know which way to go first.

Dad, ever the detective and keeping half an eye open looking for nefarious types, preferred to walk on the outside of the boardwalk, across from the shops.

Mom, however, had other ideas, thank God. So, while Dad kept on the lookout for hardened criminals, we followed Mom and proceeded to meander in and out of the boardwalk shops on her quest to find a bingo parlor. Also, if we whined enough, we knew she would buy us a treat.

There were tons of shops lining the boardwalk, in both directions. Shops where you could watch people making homemade fudge or see machines pulling salt water taffy. Others, where the smell of fresh caramel corn, had you smacking your lips. Candy, ice cream, frozen custard, hot dogs, French fries, and other marvelous concoctions to drool over was all in one place, laid out like a smorgasbord!

Lordy, this was Purgatory to four kids who were perpetually hungry, despite our parents' efforts to keep us fed.

As if that weren't enough torture, souvenir shops with great toys we just had to have were interspersed with the restaurants and food stands. You know, so you could keep up your strength while you shopped for those all important souvenirs. Stroll a few steps into a shop filled with beach balls, sunglasses, mugs, and fragrant little cedar boxes and then step next door and get a frozen custard cone. It was blissful agony mixed with rampant commercialism.

The famous boardwalk teemed with tourists strolling, tourists on bicycles, and tourists packed into trams zipping from end to end. This was the 1950's, and the Atlantic City boardwalk was still in its golden phase.

However, in a scant ten years, gambling casinos, glitzy hotels like Bally's or Trump's Taj Mahal would begin yet another incarnation in Atlantic City's life cycle.

But on this day in the summer of 1953, the regal, grand dames of the boardwalk held court and glittered in the sunlight. Hotels like the Chalfont-Haddon Hall, The Traymore, The Shelburne and The Marlborough-Blenheim reigned supreme, one more imposing than the other.

The Chalfont, loomed large with its impressive sweeping entrance. The Traymore's balconies and turrets majestically looked out over the Atlantic Ocean. The Hotel Dennis' lovely gardens, dotted with umbrella tables for diners, edged right up to the boardwalk's edge. All of these elegant hotels, with pavilions, fountains and gardens, held court and had dominated the shore line since the late 1800's. Many of them with storied histories that saw the likes of Frank Sinatra, Princess Grace of Monaco, Bob Hope and even Al Capone cross their thresholds.

Gawking like the tourist I was, I remember thinking what impressively beautiful buildings they were and wished we could go inside and see them up close. It was the first time I had ever seen such architecture because there certainly wasn't anything that grand in Allentown that I ever saw except maybe the PP & L Tower.

But Dad was not inclined to go gallivanting around the inside of toney boardwalk hotels with four rambunctious kids. It was enough to keep tabs on us trooping around the boardwalk shops.

We joined other tourists, then, strolling up and down the boardwalk, taking pictures of each other, souvenir hunting and looking for Bingo parlors for Mom, while Dad kept his restless hazel orbs trained on us and possible pick-pockets. Finally, we had lunch and hit the beach.

Hauling all of our gear — beach blankets, toys etc. just like other tourists, we joined the throngs of sun worshipers. There is something rather mesmerizing about sitting on a beach blanket and watching the waves break as the sun beats down on your body. The somnolent sound of waves can induce daydreams or even a nap. But people watching can be almost as much fun. The passing parade of bathers, who feel the need to walk back and forth on the beach, offers another pleasant diversion. Indeed, your fellow sun worshipers can provide all kinds of entertainment. I noticed that back then people seemed to be a lot skinnier. Probably from all that walking back and forth.

Of course, the boys joined other kids running back and forth to the water's edge and built castles and moats in the sand. Mom just sat back and relaxed, a rarity for her. Even Dad seemed to unwind a little. I think I actually saw him nod off for two minutes. The cop in him rarely let him relax.

After baking in the sun, a gingerly stroll to the ocean's edge over the sizzling sand was in order. I didn't know how to swim and was always afraid of the water. It took me awhile to get used to the unbalanced feeling of the waves pulling the sand from beneath my feet. But jumping the waves to cool off after baking in the hot sun was pretty great!

We spent the afternoon on the lookout for jelly fish, teeny sea horses and seashells. When we tired of that, we could just sit back and contemplate the vastness of the ocean while we tried to pick out the freighters and other ships way off on the horizon.

But finally, after a strenuous afternoon lolling on the beach and playing in the waves, the day came to a close and it was time to head back to the Chestnut Inn.

You and I, dear sister, were excited to have a room to ourselves like grownups. Mom and Dad and the boys went to their room and we headed for our promised luxurious bath.

Even though it had been a full day and we were tired, we were determined to make the most of our very own hotel room. It was just a darned shame that we didn't know about room service then, because a chocolate marshmallow peanut sundae would really have enhanced our stay.

Although, I rather doubt that the Chestnut Inn provided room service. Not to mention, Mom and Dad would have seriously murdered us if we had ordered anything.

Finally, exhausted, we hit the sheets.

Now you would think that after such a full day, we would have dropped off to sleep immediately.

Nope. Not hardly. Because weren't in bed five minutes, dear sister, when you started to bounce around and toss and turn. I waited, somewhat irritably, for you to settle.

Just when I figured you were done bouncing around, you popped up and said, "Jannie, I feel itchy."

To which I compassionately replied, "Yeah, fine, it's ok. You're not itchy. Just go to sleep."

I pounded my pillow and sighed while you continued to do the twist like Chubby Checker.

But, ah, the power of suggestion!

Because, now I too, began to toss and turn. Damned if I didn't feel itchy as well!

Finally, in desperation, we zipped across the hall to Mom and Dad and told them we couldn't sleep. They promptly sent us back to our room!

So, what was our problem? Here we were, in our very own hotel room with Mom and Dad just steps away. Were we nervous about being alone in our own room in a strange hotel? Perhaps. But there weren't any creepy noises that I could recall. Actually, for a resort town, the place was rather quiet. Hadn't we just had a nice warm, relaxing bath?

What was causing our anxiety — and more importantly, our itchiness? Was it just "all in our minds"?

Or… was something far more sinister happening? Was something else afoot, Watson? Did, mayhap, the Chestnut Inn have a few unregistered guests - *in our beds*?

Now, being the hotel lodging novices that we were, we never even heard of bed bugs. Which was a good thing, I think. Everything in our room seemed to be in order, nice and tidy. But clearly *something* was amiss. What was it?

After our curt dismissal from the room across the hall, we returned to our bed and tried for another ten minutes or so to get comfortable. No dice. Not happening.

Finally, we burst in upon Mom and Dad again, this time whining that something in our bed was making us itchy!

That's all Dad had to hear! As a world traveler, courtesy of dear old Uncle Sam and the Army Air Corp, he knew all about unregistered guests in hotel room beds.

So that night, we all ended up staying in Mom and Dad's room. Good thing we were a skinny bunch of kids. Morning dawned swiftly (but not swiftly enough) and we promptly checked out of the Chestnut Inn — never to return!

Now I know, dear reader, what you may be may be thinking. Maybe it was the soap, and that long hot bath, or perhaps the detergent the sheets or towels were laundered in or even *nerves.*

Perhaps. But we didn't stick around long enough to find out.

Nonetheless, the Chestnut Inn was inducted into the Monahan Family Hall of Fame lexicon, along with other memorable sayings and places. To us, the name Chestnut Inn became synonymous with things to be avoided and a caveat for, "Find another hotel, dude!"

See, I just knew we should have stayed at the Chalfont! Or the Traymore, or the Shelburne or the Breakers or that lovely place with the white porches, or…

Good Night, sleep tight
Don't let the bed bugs bite!

RUNAWAYS

The Monahan family generally operated like a Fortune 500 company. Ok, maybe not 500 and the fortune *was* pretty iffy. But there was never any doubt about who was in charge of the corporation. Dad was the CEO in charge of everything and Mom was the CFO in charge of the company purse strings. And I, well, being on the brink of the heady age of eleven and eldest child, I was the Administrative Assistant, aka the Overseer, kind of like Simon Legree.

While you, Jerry and Jimmy, my dear sister, made up the rest of the corporation, the *personnel*.

Mom and Dad made all the rules and always presented a united front as far as any management choices were concerned. As in any company, there were times when the *personnel* were not pleased with certain directives handed down from management. (This is where I excelled. My response generally being, "Because Dad/Mom said so, that's why!")

Complaints were duly noted. But going on strike was not an option. Plus, you kids were too young to know what a strike was anyway, and one of your numbers was always napping. This did reduce your bargaining power somewhat. In fact, any rebellions were swiftly quelled. So, the only other available choice left to the *personnel* to protest management's decisions was to create a major disturbance by threatening to leave the company.

By using this chip as leverage, *personnel* figured, both the CEO and CFO would feel so darned bad, that they would relent, change their policy (maybe even shed a few tears at their impending loss) and reconsider a new collective bargaining policy with their *personnel*.

While this particular tactic was frequently employed by certain agitators in the company, (you and Jerry) the following is an account of one particular event when management decided to remain firm!

It was a hot, humid, sultry summer day. A glaring sun hid behind hazy skies that scowled down on everything in the city! The kind of weather that makes you feel uncomfortable, irritable, crabby. When your shirt sticks to your back and the moist air is like pea soup and just breathing is an effort. When the barometer is dropping like a rock and you just can't wait for the storm to break.

But inside the little ranch house on South Leh Street, a different storm had already broken. Tempers flared. Harsh words were spoken. Drawers were banged! Doors were slammed.

However, the front office had spoken. There would be NO bargaining. The CFO was standing by the directives. (The CEO was at his day job tooling around in a police patrol car somewhere in the city but *he* had issued those directives. They were irrevocable.)

In the middle bedroom, hushed child-like voices planned a break. There were sounds of scraping in the co-conspirators' room. They too had issued *their* final decree.

They would leave the company. Again. This time, it was to be a harsh, absolute break.

Finally, a thwacking sound filled the humid air as the screen door banged shut with a blistering finality on heretofore happy lives.

The scene, as I remember it, was simply pitiful!

I watched as two little tow headed disgruntled *personnel*, one seven years of age, and the other only five, slowly wended their way down the flower lined path of their former idyllic abode. Toting a battered, ratty suitcase, they trudged up the hill at a snail's pace, leaving their cherished home/company, and meager possessions (toys, new jeans, snacks etc.) behind.

A home that did not care about them, a home that did not understand them, a home that did not value them — anymore! (Pause here for heart wrenching sobs and the distant sound of violins.)

The poor little dears took turns carting the battered old suitcase that contained all their worldly belongings (a few sets of underwear because Mom always told us you never knew when you might a need a change).

Perhaps they could make Union Street (two blocks away) by nightfall they mused. Then, maybe, a chance at a new life, someplace where they were appreciated, where they could do what *they* wanted, where they could find (sob) happiness!

Maybe, with luck, they could even make it to Marstellar's grocery store at Union Terrace Park (four blocks away not counting the lake and clearly out of their CORPORATE controlled boundary zone).

Once there, they could beg for candy. Peanuts, the proprietor, was a soft touch and goodhearted. He might spring for some free root beer barrels or Tootsie Rolls. He might heed their dire dilemma. The kindhearted, benevolent man might even be stirred enough by their misfortune to part with a bag of chips. The twenty-five cent size!

I watched their agonizingly slow progress, the tentative steps, each one carrying them further into the great unknown!

With no home, no position, no money (not that they had much anyway), they were literally out on their butts in the hot, humid, cruel world.

It was time for the Administrative Assistant to take action!

"Hey Mom, Kathy and Jerry are running away again," I dutifully snitched, er, reported, as I watched my siblings slowly walking up the sidewalk in front of our home.

"Uh, they're going up the hill towards McMullen's and this time they took a suitcase." (Yes, the corporate spy, Monahan the Mole, was on the job.)

"I know," Mom said, calmly ironing some clothes. "Keep an eye on them, will you please?"

"You betcha," I replied, warming to my 'spy task'. I slipped outside to see how far the disgruntled *personnel* had progressed. Hiding beside the arborvitae in our front yard, (scratchy smelly things), I waited to see what would happen next.

I peeked out from behind the tallest arborvitae and brushed away a spider web. Oh yuk! This spying gig did have its pitfalls.

Now, all of us kids knew what our boundaries in the neighborhood were. We pretty much had orders from Corporate on how far our neighborhood boundaries extended.

At that point, we could toddle up to Manny's house three doors away, but going past Brummel's into the next block was a definite no-no. Fairview street was totally out of bounds and don't even think about waltzing all the way up to Union Street for any reason without adult supervision!

I watched from my arborvitae hideout as the runaways reached the Corporate enforced boundary line, looked around and sat down on the curb.

"They're sitting on the curb in front of Brummel's house, Mom. Kathy's telling Jerry something," I dutifully reported back to my CFO.

Glancing at the kitchen clock, Mom calmly replied, "They'll be back for supper". She sprinkled one of Dad's shirts and steam wreathed her head as she continued her ironing.

"But just keep an eye on them please. You never know what Kathy might think of next."

The airless afternoon became stuffier, stifling away with nary a breeze to ruffle Mom's ironing, while we just waited out the runaways — Mom behind her ironing board and me in my arborvitae lair.

Occasionally I peeked out from my arborvitae hideout to observe the runaways and dutifully reported back through the open living room window to my CFO.

Just then, the phone rang. Mom answered. I listened in intently to the conversation. This is how spies gather intelligence/information. Spies had to be quiet and observant, and look non-descript (as in, don't attract any attention even when they're lurking like Boris Badenov in spider infested arborvitaes). And I have to say, I was getting pretty good at it.

This is how the phone conversation sounded, from my end anyway.

Mom - Hello.
Caller - Garble, garble, garble
Mom - Oh yes, I know. I'm quite aware. We've been watching them.

Caller - More garble, garble, garble, breath, snort, garble

Mom - Well I'm sure they don't plan on trampling your flowers or sprinkling stones on   your sidewalk. They're just sitting on the curb, planning on running away.

Caller - Garble, suitcase, worry.

Mom - Concerned? Heavens, no. They know they're not allowed to go any further up the block than Brummel's house. They'll be home for dinner. But thanks for your concern. Bye.

Wow. Even on a hot, sultry summer day, my mom was so cool! I had to hand it to her.

Because, apparently, one of the neighbors noticed the runaways and just *haaad* to call Mom to complain about them sitting on the curb. Though Mom never said who, I always figured it was probably someone who had bratty kids *she* wished *would* run away. No such luck, apparently.

The hot afternoon sweltered on and the dinner hour drew nigh. The two runaways, baked in the hazy, late afternoon sun as they sat on the curb, trying to decide their fate. The ultimate question loomed large. Dare they even think it? Should they breach the corporate controlled boundary line?

By now, they had to be starved. Monahan's never did well when they missed a meal or two. (In their anger fueled departure, the runaways neglected to take any snacks or drinks.) Plus, I am sure their skinny butts had to be sore from sitting on that concrete curb for so long.

I noticed they looked a tad worried. The enormity of their situation was clearly dawning on them.

For one thing, it's a little hard to run away when you're only allowed to go one block up the street! Kind of puts a damper on breakouts.

As the spy watched from behind our neighbor Manny's rhododendrons, (I had moved my spying position closer), the two malcontents huddled, deep in conversation. It looked like some decision was about to be made. I needed to get closer.

I couldn't hear the entire conversation, since Manny was sawing something in his garage which was kind of drowning out my intelligence gathering.

Wonder what he was fixing this time? I never saw a guy who had so much stuff to fix. I'd have to check it out on my way back to my arborvitae hideout.

Manny was a terrific neighbor and his wife Mary made the best Slovak Kolachi (cookies) I ever ate. I sniffed the air while I waited. Hmm. No kolachi. Guess Mary wasn't baking today. Too bad. That would really have enhanced my spying gig.

I edged past Manny's rhodies and was now crossing into enemy territory, Brummel's yard. We kids had absolute orders from Corporate and from the Brummel's as well, *to keep off their perfectly manicured lawn!* But technically, I was in their azalea's and not on their lawn so I figured it was all good. Also, now I could hear the runaways.

I am sure they were beginning to realize their dilemma as they reposed on the hard concrete curb. Their skinny little butts had to be killing them. Where could they go? They had reached the end of their boundary line. They had no food, no money. With only two sets of underwear between them, well, one can only imagine!

Manny started drilling something, but I was close enough to hear the conversation in between drills.

Jerry was whining, as usual. "Hey, I'm getting hungry. Plus, my butt really hurts."

"Well, stand up then," Kathy said with all the sympathy of a prison guard.

"But I'm tired. I'm thirsty too. You got anything to drink in there?" he asked, pointing to the ratty suitcase.

"No, I forgot," she sighed. "But, if we hurry, Marstellar's is still open. Maybe we can get an orange drink."

"Dad will kill us! You know we're not allowed to go that far. You got any money?"

"Me? I thought you had that candy money from Baba," she retorted.

"Uh, it's in my hiding place in my room," he responded, throwing a handful of gravel into the street.

Leaning over to tie her shoelace, Kathy sighed again.

"Can you see, is anyone coming after us?" she asked him.

"No, I don't see anybody. Mom didn't even come out," Jerry replied with a little catch in his throat. He looked forlornly down the street at the safe haven that was once his home.

This was pretty bad, from their concrete curb perspective. Could it be that no one really cared about them?

Then, like two little puppies, they sniffed the air.

"Mmm. Smells like Mary is making steak. Maybe we could go there for supper," Kathy suggested.

"Mom will kill us," he reminded her, throwing another handful of gravel into the street.

"I have an idea," Kathy said.

"What?"

"How about we go home for supper and run away tomorrow. Whaddya think?"

"Good idea," he eagerly responded.

Picking up their suitcase and rubbing their butts, they turned around and headed back down the hill towards home.

The spy beat a hasty retreat, through Manny's backyard, around Mom's veggie patch and back into the house.

"Here they come, Mom," I announced breathlessly as I plopped down on the sofa.

Toting their worldly underwear back home, the runaways appeared in the kitchen and asked that age old question.

"Hey Mom, what's for supper?"

I don't recall if any other words of recrimination were ever spoken by management.

I don't recall if any punishments were ever meted out upon the little malcontents! Probably not.

It was too hot. Plus, they suffered enough, sitting on that concrete curb.

But, you know, home is where they always take you back! And if you are lucky, it's chicken and rice night.

"Please pass the chicken, Mom. We're starving"!

THE SUMMER OF THE RESCUES

The sick, the injured and the dying. My youngest brother James was always bringing them home.

At the lower end of South Street in Hamilton Park where we lived, there were abundant fields and vacant lots all around our house, with new homes being built every day. Those fields teemed with wildlife; birds, cats, rabbits, field mice, groundhogs and the occasional possum.

The fields and vacant lots were also a veritable wonderland of adventure to four kids raised in the inner city and now let loose in the suburbs. We became intimately acquainted with sumac and poison ivy. Milkweed pods, dandelion, wild rose, various weeds and spindly silk trees begging to be climbed enhanced our outdoor experiences tenfold.

This was our first full summer in our new neighborhood since we had moved from Chew Street the year before. James was another year older now. Old enough now to join us on our forays into the wilds. He and Jerry would play all day building tree forts and tree houses in the fields behind our house. The more sinkholes and gullies there were in those fields, the better. It was a terrain worthy of Mars and some of the dirt was just as red!

But that summer, thanks to James, another diversion entered our inventive play activities.

"Hey Jan, look what I found."

James' voice rose with excitement as he ran towards me. Cupped in his pudgy hands, he held a baby sparrow. Sadly though, the tiny bird was not flying off anywhere anytime soon. It appeared to have a broken wing.

"Maybe we can fix it," he said looking up at me hopefully. James generally figured he could fix anything. Since he was not yet five, this was understandable and his latent EMT tendencies were beginning to emerge.

"Uh, I'm not sure," I replied with all the assurance of a medical student about to flunk. But we took it home and tried to feed it milk and cookies. Jerry mentioned worms, but I nixed that idea. I was not going to touch a worm. Yuk.

Alas, the poor thing expired within an hour.

So being the compassionate souls we were, we decided to have a wake and a funeral. Thus was born, The Monahan Mortuary.

We came by it honestly enough because a) we were Irish and b) one of our distant relatives actually was an undertaker. So we instinctively knew we needed to give the dearly departed a great send off.

Unfortunately, though, the wake was rather short, since we really hadn't known the dearly departed for very long.

We said kindhearted things, such as, we hoped Chip (we had to give him a name for his popsicle stick marker) had had a happy, if short, life. Whilst discussing his life, we realized that he probably got to see a lot more of Allentown than we ever did. You know, a birds-eye view, as it were. In an inspiring touch, we declared that all his bird friends were surely going to miss him and would probably chirp a few tunes in his honor.

Then we found a small sparrow size box, one of Mom's good cleaning rags (nothing but the best from the Monahan Mortuary) and proceeded to send good old Chip off to his eternal reward in grand Irish style.

After saying more really nice things about the deceased, and following my St. Joseph's Missal, we decided that we should probably sing a hymn. Since we really didn't know Chip's religious affiliation, we sang "Over the Rainbow", figuring he probably got to fly over there from time to time, just like it said in the song.

All in all, it was a grand funeral.

Apparently James thought so too. Because once he realized how much fun it could be, he went on the hunt looking for more critters in various stages of terminality, rather like an undertaker in Tombstone.

But there was method to James' madness. Secretly, he just wanted a pet. So by literally beating the bushes, he figured sooner or later he would find one.

Sadly though, the only ones he ever found were either sick, injured or on their way to their eternal reward. But, I am sure in his little four and a half year old brain, there was always the hope that somehow a miracle would occur and he could fix whatever was wrong with his latest find and thus, we would have a pet. Since Mom had decreed "no pets" on more than one occasion, we figured if we found one, *surely* she would let us keep it.

A few weeks went by and one day, after a morning spent playing cowboys and Indians in the fields behind our house, he hit pay dirt. He found a little gray and white kitten.

"Look, Jan. Look what I found."

He cuddled the poor little beastie in his arms. Initially, I figured James had finally found his pet. That's when I noticed the wound on the kitten's grey and white head. I just didn't know how to tell James that the poor thing was literally on its last legs.

But James wanted to fix it, so we tried. Warm milk, Band Aids, a cozy bed and lots of petting. The four of us got kind of attached to Puff and hoped maybe at last we would finally have a pet. Sadly, Puff lasted but a day and a half, despite our medical ministrations.

In view of the fact that Puff lasted considerably longer than Chip, we decided he deserved to get the premium package offered by The Monahan Mortuary.

Firstly, he got a bigger box. (Well he *was* bigger than Chip and we knew him longer.) Then he was tenderly wrapped in an old, but clean, blue doll blanket. After burial preparations were completed, our somber funeral procession moved gravely to the back of the yard, where once again we held another Irish wake.

In the day and a half we had known him, poor little Puff had touched all of our hearts. So we spoke in hushed, reverent tones about our dearly departed friend, who had never really had a chance at life. We railed against life's unfairness, in cutting his life short. Lamenting about how he would never have a chance to play with balls of wool, pounce on fake mice or enjoy catnip. How he would never sit in our bow window taking a sunbath. Or ever enjoy another bowl of milk.

Maintaining our somber demeanor, we then moved onto the prayerful part of the service.

We began with several Our Father's, some Glory Be's and a couple of 'shineuponya's'. (May perpetual light *shine upon you*, for those of you who are unacquainted with prayers for the departed.)

Finally we concluded the premium service with the hymn, Amazing Grace. Although, when we got to the words 'a wretch like me' we stopped singing and just hummed the rest. I didn't think Puff would have liked being called a 'wretch'. He didn't live long enough to be one.

The service ended with our four collective heads bowed in a suitable display of grief.

In the weeks following Puff's departure from our lives, there was a succession of little critters that James continued to rescue that summer. Though hope seemed to spring eternal in the four and a half year old's heart, his efforts always seem to end in a funeral. But he never really gave up. He was determined to save his little friends — and acquire a pet.

Summer fell into Fall. The days grew colder and we spent less time prowling the fields. We hadn't held a funeral in weeks. In fact, we pretty much had given up on the pet rescue idea and The Monahan Mortuary closed its doors (or in our case - boxes) for good. Also, before long, the ground would be frozen, somewhat limiting our burial capability.

Then a miracle happened.

We had just come home from a shopping excursion when a teeny blue parakeet flew into the house from out of nowhere.

Mom caught it and put it under her colander while we cooed and talked to it so it would stay calm. A quick trip to the pet store and Tweetie (Ok, so we weren't so creative with names) had a new cage, a mirror and some birdie toys.

James was overjoyed. He finally had a pet. The little parakeet seemed to be in great health. No EMT needed here. Tweetie sang and twittered and tweeted, entertaining us all. Mom didn't seem to mind us having a pet like Tweetie because our Grammie always had a canary or two in a cage in *her* kitchen.

Now James could enjoy his newfound buddy. We were finally out of the funeral business. James could concentrate on other pursuits and I didn't have to constantly deliver the news that his rescues were half dead. Pretty much a win-win situation, I figured.

But one night at dinner, I found out the kid still had a hand in the funeral business.

We had just finished dinner and were waiting to see if Dad would eat his dessert. If he chose to pass it up, our forks would appear like the four musketeer's swords whipped from their scabbards and we'd all get part of a second dessert.

Dad dug into his strawberry shortcake and we collectively sighed while he smirked. If you can smirk while eating strawberry shortcake!

Suddenly James slid off of his chair and went over to stand in front of Dad. I recognized that look. That kind, compassionate expression James always reserved for our premium package funerals. Solemnity, mixed with just a pinch of sympathy and an ounce or two of concern for the bereaved.

"What the devil is he up to?", I wondered. He hadn't rescued anything in weeks. I watched as Dad munched and smirked looking down at James.

With his little hands behind his back, James solemnly approached Dad.

Looking up at the dessert poacher, James stretched out his right fist, and with an air of pride, opened it. In his small palm rested a twinkly limestone, probably gleaned from his diggings on a pretend trip to Panama.

Then in his gravest, most funereal voice, he intoned, "This is for you Daddy. It's for your gravestone!" He dropped the stone on Dad's plate.

Dad gulped, almost choking on a strawberry.

When Mom squeaked trying to suppress a laugh, James turned and threw himself into her lap.

"Oh, please don't cry, Mommy," he implored, totally misinterpreting her squeak.

Being the benevolent little soul he was, he didn't want Mom to feel left out. He reached up and opened his other fist. Of course, nestled inside was another limestone rock.

"Look! I didn't forget you Mommy. I've got one for you too," he assured her in his most somber and melancholy funeral manner.

I looked over at Mom. She was trying so hard not to laugh, that tears were falling down her cheeks. Dad was red faced and snorkeling into his napkin.

Jerry and Kathy just looked dumbfounded.

I was just wishing there was more shortcake.

Well, Fall swirled and danced into winter and rescues were curtailed. James was now onto other pursuits, like snow fort architecture and sledding. When spring came, so did baseball, fishing and bike riding. James was growing up and moving with the big boy crowd, like his brother.

But, dear reader, just in case you were wondering — no, James did *not* grow up to become a funeral director. Although, *I* think he missed his true calling. He could always muster up a concerned countenance and knew how to reassure people whenever necessary.

What he *did* become, though, was even better. He grew into a person who always felt compassion and made time to help those in need.

As a young EMT, he finally put his rescue talents to good use and helped people when they needed it most.

OFF WE GO
INTO THE WILD BLUE YONDER

Sugar jets,
They make you ---- jet propelled!!

Are you kidding me? For pity's sake, just what were you and Jerry thinking?

Personally, I never really cared for Sugar Jets, or any cereal other than Rice Krispies. At least all the Krispies did was talk back to you. But make you jet-propelled, commme on! Give me a break!

Ah, but I am getting ahead of myself, dear sister. Let's go back a little, shall we.

It was late summer as I recall, and we had been in our new house on Leh Street for a few weeks. The new grass was growing in and still roped off from trampling trespassers such as ourselves and our new friends in the neighborhood. No matter. There was plenty to do in the fields surrounding our house. And, apparently, on our back porch!

One thing about the Monahan kids, we could always find something to do to have fun. It seemed to me our feverish brains were usually working overtime, much to our poor Mother's consternation. Perhaps it was the stimulation of the cereal we ate? All those healthy, nutritious grains, Vitamin D and *sugar*!

Anyway, while I was most likely doing chores, and being a model pre-teen, you and Jerry were sloshing back Sugar Jets cereal, and scraping your bowls like famine victims.

Since I didn't care for the stuff and at least you were both out of my hair for a while, it was all good. Personally, I didn't care if you ate the whole box and drank the whole carton of milk. I had already had my breakfast, and I didn't see the big attraction for the junk. At least not at that point, I didn't. That was to come later.

I did notice on one of my passes through the living room with a dust cloth, that the two of you seemed pretty engrossed in the TV while said cereal sloshing was going on. I should have stopped to see why. Just looked like another episode of 'Sky King' to me. Besides, I couldn't stop my dusting. I think there may have been a new dress riding on it or maybe ballerina flats, or that blue crew neck sweater at Hess's that I had my eye on.

But somewhere along the line, the cereal bowls hit the sink and there were sounds of furtive whispering. Hmm. Schemes were being hatched and where you two were concerned that was never good.

I decided to stick around and observe. (I really should have become a detective. Or maybe a spy, or…never mind.)

I sat down and watched the end of 'Sky King' and then a commercial for Sugar Jets cereal came on. It was eye opening to say the very least. I had never paid it much mind before now.

Two kids, dressed in cowboy outfits, were moseying along through a fake desert on the backs of two donkeys. As they moseyed, they sang, "I'm hungry, I'm hungry…for sugar jets, good oats and wheat" whilst headed for the chuck wagon. Even the donkeys were in on it, as they swayed back and forth in time to the music.

In the background an announcer can be heard extolling the virtues of the cereal as "real food" that gives you "super" energy.

After knocking back a few spoonfuls of the stuff, our little donkey riding darlings continue to praise the "good oats and wheat", while promising their young audience that they will have great gobs of energy.

Finally, as further proof of their claims, the two kids suddenly dismounted their donkey pals, and jumped into the air, taking off into the great blue beyond, just like the Man of Steel.

Flying side by side, as fluffy white clouds slid by, the little dears clutched boxes of sugar jets cereal to their chests, chanting "Sugar jets, they make you feel like you're jet propelled."

But, I still didn't quite get it, even when I heard the two of you rummaging around in the linen closet. Should I yell at the two of you? Nah! I'd rather wait and see what you were up to.

I grabbed a magazine and went out onto our new patio.

It wasn't too long after that when the morning's entertainment picked up considerably. The two of you came out the back door. You were both wearing bath towels pinned to your shoulders with Mom's clothespins. I watched in utter fascination for a few seconds trying to figure out what in the world…

Then before I could say "Put those towels back", the two of you leaped into the air and fell off the back-porch steps. A distance of about two feet, as I recall, but far enough to crack your craniums, or break a limb. Because, you two nimrods were landing on concrete.

Well, of course, you both fell to earth faster than Icarus and his flaming feather wings.

But undaunted, and after some sort of consultation, you both got up and tried the same stunt again. Only this time, the two of you yelled in unison, "Sugar Jets, they make you jet propelled!" like some sort of magic incantation designed to lift you off the porch and propel you both into the air.

It didn't work.

After about the third try, well, it became painfully obvious to me (and I wasn't doing the jumping) that neither of you were flying off to anywhere, Sugar Jets, towel capes or not.

Even worse, you were both beginning to realize you had been 'had' — by singing kids, swaying donkeys, a cute little jingle and a slick team of Madison Avenue advertising execs. A bitter pill to swallow at your tender ages, especially after swilling all that cereal.

Man, I can still see you and Jerry, stomping back into the house, hot and sweaty and probably stuffed to the gills with cereal, muttering, **"Boy, what a crummy gyp!"**

Apparently, both you, dear sister, and Jerry actually believed the glib television advertising for Sugar Jets and decided to take Madison Avenue at its word (an oxymoron in itself).

Plus, I am sure all this preoccupation with flying came from the beginning of the program which began with the dramatic proclamation, "Out of the clear blue of the western sky comes SKY KING" as King's plane, Songbird, swoops at the camera.

Indeed, I'm sure the commercial which showed those two kids stoking up on the sugar-coated concoction and then jetting off into the wild blue yonder like Superman got the two of you thinking — and planning.

But I think a closer look at the commercial would have been in order. With, perhaps, more attention being paid to the slick (and legal department vetted) "Madison Avenue Mantra",

> Sugar Jets,
> They make you *feel like you're* jet-propelled!

GOTCHA!

SNOWSTORM

It started with a few wispy flakes of snow, just fluttering down, down, down like goose feathers from a pillow. Nothing to worry about. Just a dusting, hardly covering anything. But then, those flakes started to get bigger and came faster and faster. Unceasing flakes that continued with no promise of ending anytime soon. By morning they had covered everything with a soft, fluffy, white blanket.

We had just moved into our little ranch house that summer and now winter was upon us. This was the first snowstorm of the season, and it was promising to be a whopper, what we now refer to as a good 'old fashioned' snow storm. Old fashioned, yes, but there was nothing 'good' about it. It had snowed all night and the whole day and now night was falling. And so was more snow.

Although, watching the snow pile up in drifts against the house and seeing the streets and curb disappear under that fluffy white mantle, meant no school for us. So that was pretty good. Actually, we were socked in. There was no traffic moving anywhere that we could see in our suburban neighborhood. From the looks of things, it would be a long time till the snow plows could get us out. We weren't on a high priority list. It could be days, or even weeks, maybe! Ok, maybe not weeks, but a few days, at least!

This was going to be way different than snow on Chew Street. For one thing, we now had a cool hill to ride our sleighs on and no trolley cars or delivery trucks to worry about. Plus, we also had a back yard big enough to make a snow fort and who knows what else. Maybe the snow wouldn't get all black with cinders and mushy with truck traffic like it did on Chew Street.

After our move from the inner city to the suburbs during the summer we were so busy getting settled in and discovering our new neighborhood, we hadn't even given snow a thought. Until now.

When we awoke to the wispy white winter wonderland, the four of us could not wait to get out into the stuff. We tore through the basement looking for our sleds and boots.

Zipping around all day on our sleds with the other neighborhood kids, we had a blast. Man, this *was* way different than Chew Street.

Even the bitter cold and snow stinging our faces didn't deter us from our important work of building a snow fort. After all, we could run back into the house to warm up, dry our clothes, have hot cocoa and then go back out when we were warm and dry again. No worries about traffic or cinders to muck up our fun. We could barely contain ourselves and we played in the snow until dark.

But I guess I was growing up, because that winter, on that bitter cold, snowy night, I got a glimpse of the real world, and what snowstorms meant, at least as far as our parents were concerned.

You know, the human memory is a truly miraculous thing.

In today's world of split-second technology, we are bombarded daily with information and events — at school, at work, and at home. As time marches on though, our memories will sometimes fog up reality. But every now and again, an event occurs that time will not erase, that lays waiting in the recesses of our minds for us to rediscover, like a treasure.

These little vignettes are stored somewhere in our mental treasure troves, to be taken out and enjoyed like pictures in an album. For each of us, they are different. There seems to be no rhyme or reason why we remember the things that we do. In fact, some memories seem so insignificant, you have to wonder why they hang around at all. Yet, sometimes a smell or a casually spoken word can awaken even the most trivial of memories.

For myself, one particular vignette remains with me to this day, one that had a profound effect on me.

So, I will describe to you, my dear sister, the tiny snippet from my mental treasure trove, a memory picture that I still hold in my heart and cherish. Because it spoke volumes to me about sacrifice and made me begin to appreciate how special our dad was.

As darkness fell that night, the snow had turned fine and harsh. Like old man weather gave us the fun stuff first, and now he was getting mean and nasty with an "I'll show you!" attitude. No more Mr. Nice Flakes. Now the house was being assaulted with stinging slaps of icy snow crystals that continued to pile up in drifts.

The city was pretty much crippled by this time. There was no traffic moving anywhere — not on Leh Street, where we lived, or South Street or Fairview Street or too many other streets around the city.

After an afternoon of romping in the white stuff, we were actually enjoying a cozy evening in our new little ranch house. Dad played his Hi Fi record player and read while we played games with Mom. Occasionally a gust of wind pelted the windows of the tiny ranch with the icy crystals, like some imp throwing handfuls of sand.

But we remained comfortable and secure in our sturdy little house. Let the snow blow, gust or whatever else it wanted, we were safe and together.

Suddenly the phone rang, the harsh jangling disturbing our homey, contented evening. There was an emergency. Dad had to go into work.

Really? Now? Who in God's name goes out on a night like this?

Of course, the answer to that is 'first responders,' and Dectective Monahan was one. So, who would need detecting in a howling blizzard?

Well, there are all kinds of emergencies and that's why we need first responders. Policemen, just like firemen and EMT's, are trained for all kinds of situations.

Like rescuing the air head who went up onto his roof to fix his TV antenna in a thunder storm. Or the wing nut who just had to have a fresh pack of ciggies during a major flood. Or the young parents whose child is gravely ill and they need help getting to the hospital. Or the poor, elderly soul who has run out of life-saving medicine, to name just a few.

I remember thinking, "For pete's sake, how is Dad supposed to get to work? The car is buried in almost five feet of snow drifts and so is the street." In fact, the last time I looked out at the intersection, it seemed the snow had drifted even deeper at the bottom of the hill. A car could get lost in that frozen quagmire until spring.

A soft murmur of parental voices emanated from the kitchen. Being the nosy kid I always was, I crept closer to the kitchen. I'm sure you've heard that old saying, "children should be seen but not heard." Well I firmly held to the belief that "children should hear without being seen." (It almost always worked for me.)

I heard Mom say quietly, "Oh Gerald, do you have to go *now*?"

"They're trying to get a grader down Fairview Street and I'll walk up to meet it," he softly replied. Then, as if to rub salt in the wound, or in this case snow, the wind picked up, hurling more snow, rattling the window panes.

I crawled up on the back of the sofa and looked out the front bay window again, my face pressed against the glass, my warm breath fogging the windows. The snow drifted in piles on top of our cars and against the trees. At one point it was like a whiteout, before we called them that. I could barely make out Berlinger's house across the street.

Then I went to the side window and looked up to Fairview Street. It was dark and forbidding looking. A weak pool of light from the utility pole marked the intersection as the steadily falling snow swirled around its bottom. No cars, no movement, no plow. Zip! Nada!

It didn't take Dad all that long to get ready. Another phone call now confirmed, the plow was on the way.

I watched him trudge out the front door and clomp down the walkway to the street. The snow was up to his waist. It took him awhile just to get down our pathway and into the street where he almost disappeared. He sort of waded through the intersection, as though he was swimming in white jello. I watched as his arms swung back and forth while he tried to keep himself balanced. We kids all watched at the window then, taking turns giving Mom a step by step breakdown on his progress.

"He's gone past Berlinger's house now. Ok, there he goes, up the street. Oh wait, where is he? I can't see him," Jerry said.

A gust of snow whirled around like a mini-tornado blocking our view. "No, there he goes. I can see him holding onto his hat, Mom. Geez, it must be super windy. He's going straight up the middle of the street. He's almost at

Fairview now, Mom.   Man, the snow looks even deeper there!" I said in a hushed awestruck voice.

As we watched Dad's slow progression up South Street toward Fairview Street, we saw flickering red and yellow lights between the houses on Fairview, playing off the snow. The plow had finally made it to the intersection.

Probably to the great consternation of the folks in the next block of Fairview Street, the plow picked up Dad, turned around and headed back the way it came. After all, it came just for him!

"It came, Mom, it came, there's the plow. Oh wow, it's turning around now, there it goes, back up the hill!" Jimmy said.

We watched as the blinking red and yellow lights slowly receded into the snowy blankness.

For now, our little bit of drama and excitement was over. That was it. The plow was gone with Dad aboard, traveling slowly back up Fairview to Union Street and then on out to Hamilton Street and into center city or wherever the emergency was.

Now, the snow began to drift over the ruts as though the plow had never even been there. It had already filled in Dad's torturous path through the intersection.

But I remember feeling bereft that night after he left. The picture in my mind is still so clear. I can still see Dad, wading through that snow in the intersection in front of our house, swinging his arms with nothing to hold onto for support.

He wore a three-quarter length grey jacket, his red flannel shirt underneath, wool slacks and his high black rubber boots with clamps. And, of course, his brown felt hat tipped down over his eyes, the one that always made him look like one of Elliot Ness's 'G' men!

Lord, he had to be half frozen by the time he reached the plow. I don't think he even owned thermal underwear and probably wouldn't have worn them if he did.

Yes, I felt sad that night. Depressed that he had to leave his home on such a bitter cold evening when everyone else in the neighborhood was safe and warm with their families.

But he was needed. That was his job. It wasn't the first time and would not be the last time duty called.

Of course, now that I am older, I do understand. Yet, I still often wonder about my dad, the policeman.

How many times as a young patrolman on a lonely three A.M. beat did he whistle a comforting tune?

How many times did he enter a warehouse with service revolver drawn in search of thieves?

How many times did the midnight darkness stand between him and furtive noises at the end of a blind alley?

How many times did he stand, with head bowed, as sheet draped bodies were removed from a home where life had gone terribly wrong?

Now, even all these years later, when it snows and the wind taps its icy fingers against my window panes, the sound awakens those snowy memories and takes me back to that night so many years ago.

I see a small pool of pale light from the utility pole outside our little ranch house. It just barely illuminates the snow filled intersection as a man treks through waist deep snow. He is trudging through the freezing drifts alone, passing snug homes, warmly lit from within, whose occupants are completely unaware of his passing.

But this man moves with purpose. He has a job to do. It is important.

I see myself as I was then, a little ten-year old girl with her face pressed to the cold window, watching her father navigate the wintry landscape in a stinging snow storm.

Yes, I know lots of ten-year olds think that their fathers were heroes.

But mine really was one

THE BALLAD OF HAJJI BABA
OR THE COUSINS LAMENT!

Back when we were kids it was often the custom to visit relatives on Sundays. It didn't cost anything to take a family of six out visiting, other than gas for the car and that was relatively cheap in those days.

In fact, we did this fairly regularly. After Mass, we would all pile into the car and motor on up to Northampton to visit with Grandpop and Baba (Grammie). Usually, our cousins, Denny and Pat would be there too and we would have a great time running around Baba's big old house on Washington Avenue, while furtively making plans for the rest of the day.

After tiring out the grandparents, it was on to our cousins' house, (Aunt Polly and Uncle Bill) in Catasauqua where we were "just going to make a quick stop". However, this generally turned into a long fun-filled afternoon.

On days when it was really cold outside, as it was on this particular dreary November Sunday, the first thing we kids did when we went into their house was stand on the heating grate between the living room and dining room after Uncle Billy stoked the furnace in the basement.

Toasting ourselves like marshmallows until we started to melt, we then turned our attention to more important matters. Playtime! Watching TV was't even an option when there were so many other things to do at their house.

Sometimes we would play in their yard running up and down a small embankment that was like a roller coaster hill or we would put one of us in a wagon and push it down the hill making our own roller coaster. Being the inventive thinkers that we were, we would make up all kinds of games. Some involved races, Simon says, cowboys and Indians, or just throwing a ball back and forth, since their yard was long and narrow.

However, if it was too inclement to play in the yard, we hung out in the front living room playing indoor games.

Our folks would then gather in the kitchen and begin to play cards, and occasionally our Aunt Kitty would join them. Our function, while this activity transpired, was to lay low and not cause any trouble. This was an awesome responsibility and an impossible task, from our kids' point of view.

In fact, the trip to Catty (as locals called the town), was preceded by this warning from our parents. From Mom, "now don't make a mess" and from Dad, "see that you all behave yourselves or else". (There was always an "or else" and we were canny enough to make sure we never learned what it could be).

However, dear sister, it was on one of those memorable occasions, when we discovered what the "or else" was. It was all Nat King Cole's fault.

Nat was, at the time, one of Mom's favorite singers. He had just made a record called "Hajji Baba", a catchy little ditty that was zipping up the charts. We would sing the chorus over and over, because mostly you just repeated Hajji, Hajji, Hajji, Hajji Baba. Quite easy for us to remember.

Nat would appear on television wearing long desert robes with his head swathed in a turban. Then, he and his chorus would proceed to sing "Hajji, Hajji, Hajji, Hajji Hajji Baaaaba", which was also known as the Persian Lament! (Bear with me here and you"ll soon find out why.)

Anyway, Mom loved that song! It *was* rather catchy. Why you could almost see the camels plodding their way across rivers of sand to a desert fortress with minarets and turrets while Nat crooned in that smooth, mellow voice of his!

On this particular dreary, wet, November Sunday, the folks sat down in the kitchen to play cards as usual. Playing outside in the yard was out and we had exceeded board games, bypassed names games and any other games we could think up, so now we were bored and getting a bit noisy.

From the kitchen at the back of house came the stern command, "You kids go upstairs to play and *keep quiet*." Really! Six kids! Keep Quiet! What were they thinking?

Apparently, a hot, penny-ante poker game was in progress and the folks couldn't concentrate with all the thumping and giggling going on in the front room. Plus, I am sure they figured we would be two stories up and they wouldn't be disturbed. Ha, the poor misguided souls.

Since we didn't need an engraved invitation, all six of us scrambled up the stairs to Denny's attic bedroom on the third floor, with whoops and giggles receding up the stairs with us.

Denny's bedroom was just the ticket for this dismal afternoon. Tucked under the eaves, with slanting ceilings and two little curtained windows on the side, the room was furnished with a double bed, a wardrobe, a dresser and a cedar chest.

"What are all those walnuts doing here?" I asked, eyeing the English walnuts spread out on towels all over the floor.

"Mom's drying them for the nut rolls," Denny replied. Ah yes, walnuts that would later be turned into a scrumptious filling for the famous nut rolls that Aunt Polly made for the Christmas holidays.

Skirting the drying walnuts, we eased over to his bed, the six of us plopping down to discuss our next play option. (No, there was not a TV in Denny's room, or a phone, or computer, etc.)

This meant we had to *use our imaginations*. Several suggestions were made and then discarded as being unfeasible. Trampoline on the bed, umm, too noisy. Hide and seek, umm, nowhere to hide. Statues, no place to spin around. Simple Simon, we needed more room. We were quiet for about two seconds while we continued to ponder this dilemma.

I can't quite remember who floated the idea of having a "show". (Oh, alright. I'll come clean. It was me!) Since I took dancing lessons and had appeared in some noteworthy productions, I was looking forward to using my creative side. Happily, for me, on this particular day, I had a ready-made star (not me) and captive audience, so to speak.

"Hey, ya know, we could have a show," I announced. "This could be our stage," I pointed at the space in front of Denny's bed, "and this could be audience seating," I gestured toward the bed. Our excitement grew as the idea took shape. I was always pretty good at ginning up a crowd.

Ah yes, just like an earlier backyard extravaganza on Chew Street, my incarnation of Max Bialystock, that brilliant Broadway producer, was back with a vengeance! It was show time!

"I could do a dance," piped Kathy. "I could be a ballerina."

"Ooo and I can twirl my baton and march," volunteered Pat, the future majorette of Catty High.

Then Jerry and Jim joined the Greek chorus of wannabee actors.

"Yeah, we wanna be in it too, Jannie", they sang. God alone knew what they had in mind for a performance.

"Uh, well, how about later. For now, you can all just be part of the audience," I said. "After all, the audience is just as important, you know," I reasoned, trying to mollify them.

I had to nip this potential revolt in the bud, pronto. The last thing I needed was for Jerry and Jim to join the fracas too, totally ruining my imminent production. Ideas were already buzzing around in my brain and I didn't need the two of them to gum it up.

"Remember, we're supposed to be quiet," I reminded my would-be audience.

Besides, it had already been decided by Max (me), that Denny would be the star performer. (I knew raw talent when I saw it.)

You, dear sister, and Jerry, Jim and Pat, would be our audience. I, of course, was once again on call as the producer, director, costumer, announcer, etc., etc.

"Uh, what about all those walnuts," Denny pointed out, looking around the floor.

He was right. The walnuts had to go. They were in our way. For one thing, the stage needed to be prepared. Also, we needed the towels they were laying on for Denny's costume.

"Hmm. Let's see. How about we push some over here, and look, there's room beside the bed," I instructed. We all got to work pushing them aside here and there. We could gather them up in no time later on, we figured.

The big production quickly began to take shape. Denny and I installed our audience in the theater seating area (Denny's bed) and reminded them to be quiet while we got the stage ready. Plus, we didn't want you kids mucking around in the walnuts.

Once we had our stage prepared and the walnuts stowed, sort of, I began to lay out the show. After measuring the room, I decided that Denny would make his grand entrance from behind the wardrobe. This left a nice large area in front of the seating area (bed) for the actual stage.

Late afternoon shadows began to darken the room, so Denny turned on the dresser lamps. Lo and behold, being the resourceful darlings that we were, it rapidly became apparent that the little lamps would make great spot lights.

"You know what would be good. It would be neat if we had something to cover them with," I suggested.

"I know just what," said Pat jumping off of the bed and scurrying down to her bedroom. The sound of drawers scraping, closing and banging, floated up the attic stairs. Pretty soon she returned with a red silk scarf of her mom's.

Wrapping it around one of the lamps, I found it produced a nice warm, reddish glow and left the top of the lamp open for the spotlight part. The effect was quite nifty, actually and I could now add lighting director to my growing list of credentials.

Meanwhile, as Pat monkeyed around with the spotlight, I took my star backstage (behind the wardrobe) and had him dress in robes and towels.

Adjusting his wardrobe, I could hear the beginnings of "noises off." It seemed our audience was becoming a bit restive due to anticipation of the coming theatricals. After I yelled a few "knock it off's", proper decorum resumed in the audience and we were almost ready to proceed.

Now, with the audience re-seated (somewhat anxiously), and the spotlight swathed in red silk, my new star was eager to make his grand entrance.

It was Showtime!

The opening (and *only)* starring number was to be (drum roll here), you guessed it — Hajji Baba! The audience bounced and squirmed eagerly in their theater/bed seats. The spotlight came up and panned the room. Then, in my best announcer voice, I began.

"And now, ladies and gentlemen, here to sing his recent hit, "Hajji Baba", straight from a sold-out engagement at the Twilight Room in New York City, yes, here is our star, that renowned singing artist, "Denny O"Donnell"!

I hit the wardrobe with our nifty spotlight and Denny emerged from the darkened wall behind the wardrobe to screams and yells from our delighted spectators.

He bobbed up and down in his Arab robes like he was riding a camel across the desert, all the while singing mellifluously, "Hajji, Hajji, Hajji, Hajji, Hajji Baba! Hajji Baba!" (Yeah, I know there were a lot of Hajji's in there.)

The audience went wild! His melodic tones filled the attic bedroom. I must say, he *did* sing beautifully. Almost as good as Nat. (Ha! I knew raw talent when I heard it.)

"Hear my lament, oh my beloved," he sang as the spotlight shadowed his movements. Then he swung around with his robes and towels and proceeded to go back and forth in front of the bed whilst the red spotlight followed him.

"Hajji, Hajji, Hajji," he intoned. My "star" was really getting into the spirit of Hajji.

In fact, he "wowed" the audience. Like all great performers, the more his audience screamed and cheered and encouraged him, the better and more captivating his performance became. In fact, the lighting director was having a little trouble keeping up with him.

The electrically charged performance had an immediate and profound effect on our audience of four.

"Hajji, Hajji, Hajji!" they yelled. The audience was now up on their knees, then up on their feet, then jumping up and down, up and down (on the bed) cheering, yelling, clapping for good old Hajji. Why it was absolutely transfixing!

Then the unforeseen, the unanticipated, the unimaginable—happened.

Because, right in the middle of Hajji's fourth pass through the desert, a thundering, horrendous crash filled the attic air!

Our audience now found themselves on the floor rolling around on a collapsed bed with English walnuts rolling all over them.

However, downstairs in the kitchen, it must have sounded like the roof just caved in. Because, before we could say "holy crap, somebody fix the bed", the parents were already hotfooting it up the stairs, followed by Aunt Kitty.

You know, I never realized Mom and Dad could move that fast. And Uncle Bill and Aunt Polly were right behind them.

The scene that greeted them must have looked like something out of bedlam. Walnuts were rolling around everywhere, and Denny was red in the face and sweaty from his turban (which was now half draped around his neck). You kids were sprawled out all over the floor (still giggling), the curtains were askew (don't have a clue how that happened) and I was caught red silk scarf handed, so to speak, with our spotlight.

Oh brother, were Mom and Dad ticked! The yelling was loud and immediate. As I recall, it went something like this.

"What the devil were you kids thinking, what did you do, how *could* you have done all that (actually it was pretty easy), and Omigod, just look at the room, how will we ever fix the bed, etc, etc, etc?"

There *were* a few weak "Oh, I'm sure they didn't mean it's" from Aunt Kitty. (Childless, she could always be counted on to take our side.) But with all the hollering, no one else heard her.

The yelling went on for quite a while. All six of us received a pretty brutal dressing down. However, I don't recall any corporal punishment being meted out, although we did have to clean up Denny's room before we left and beg Aunt Polly's and Uncle Bill's forgiveness for destroying their house. Also, I think a new red scarf may have been mentioned. (Guess I'd have to work that one off, since I never got an allowance.)

The ride home was a quiet one (after Dad and Mom quit yelling). The two of them really were equal opportunity disciplinarians. When Mom finished, Dad started. Mom would start with that refrain which went something like this, "And another thing" and then Dad would jump in with "Oh and that reminds me", so we got the devil twice. Good thing it was only a seven-mile trip home.

Now, you would think that after being "read the riot act" by two sets of parents, our natural exuberance would have been somewhat curtailed. That being scolded for such reckless and irresponsible behavior would have dampened our enthusiasm for future play dates.

Even *after* the inevitable threats were made, like "It'll be a cold day in (a very hot place) before you get to play there again!" and "Aren't you all ashamed of yourselves for your behavior?"

Answer — No, not in the least. Just sorry the bed collapsed because up until then we were having a whiz bang time.

Besides, it didn't take us long to recognize those were just empty threats anyway. How did we know this? Well, we soon figured out that our parents wanted to play cards as much as we wanted to visit with our cousins.

After all, in our world, Sundays were for our relatives, our family, our kith and kin. Where else *would* we go on a Sunday?

And, bedroom demolition aside, we continued to do just that for many years to come.

But, I will never forget one dreary, wet, Sunday afternoon long ago, when the Ballad of Hajji Baba filled a cozy attic bedroom while six little cousins had a ball!

Hajji, Hajji, Hajji, Hajji, Hajji Baba, Hajji Baba,

He was always in love, in love, in love ....

Nat King Cole
Ned Washington-Dimitri Tiomkin

ACKNOWLEDGEMENTS

I want to thank my family and friends for their gracious support and help over the past year in helping to prepare *Chew Street and Beyond* for publication.

Especially a great big "Thank You" to all my *readers* who spent hours searching for typos, inaccuracies etc.

To my sister, Kathy Weiss and dear friend, Mary Teresa Kloss, readers extraordinaire. Your words of support and encouragement mean the world to me.

To my sister-in-law and friend, Pat Monahan, my literature, grammar and punctuation expert who never missed a misplaced comma or weird syntax, my unending gratitude.

To my husband, my go to guy for weird questions, like do you remember the trolley route in Fullerton and that cute little shack at the halfway stop or how do you put a set of chains on a truck — screw, snap or clip? It just gets better!

To my daughter, Candice Pasco, for always providing the encouraging word and talking up *Letters* to anyone who would listen, you are marvelous.

Finally, to my daughter, Ann Margaret Longenbach, who had the enormous task of preparing the text for downloading, deleting my numerous 'ands', and also listening to my whining, I couldn't do this without you.

My love and gratitude to all of you.

ABOUT THE AUTHOR

Janice Monahan Rodgers lives in Northampton, Pennsylvania with her husband and one finicky rescued tuxedo cat. She has two lovely daughters and enjoys writing for children. You can contact her via email, jmrodgersauthor@gmail.com or visit her website at

https://janicemonahanrodgers.com

Besides personal memoirs, Mrs. Rodgers also has several children's books in process, targeted for 2018 publication. Look for *The Red Cape Caper*, first book in *The Circus Mysteries* series, a children's chapter book, soon.